THE FINAL SCORE

Dennis Mark

PublishAmerica
Baltimore

© 2007 by Dennis Mark.
All rights reserved. No part of this book may be reproduced, stored in a retrieval system or transmitted in any form or by any means without the prior written permission of the publishers, except by a reviewer who may quote brief passages in a review to be printed in a newspaper, magazine or journal.

First printing

All characters appearing in this work are fictitious. Any resemblance to real persons, living or dead, is purely coincidental.

At the specific preference of the author, PublishAmerica allowed this work to remain exactly as the author intended, verbatim, without editorial input.

ISBN: 1-4241-6376-5
PUBLISHED BY PUBLISHAMERICA, LLLP
www.publishamerica.com
Baltimore

Printed in the United States of America

To W.H. and Bobby, the two most fair men I have ever known.

The Final Score

Robert McGuire sat at a table in the rear of the bar. This was the position he normally took anytime he found himself in this type of situation. He had already ordered his drink and with cigarette lit, he waited while mentally adding up everyone he saw. He was looking for his next mark. He always found the right person. You know the type, plenty of money and just a little short on brains. The guy who was looking to make a fast and easy buck and really did not care what it took to accomplish this desire just as long as it was indeed accomplished and to hell with the consequences. Robert knew he would find the right person, it just took time.

As the waitress arrived with his drink, she was trying to engage her newest costumer in at least some small talk. She was good looking, and knew it, and used her looks to warm up the coldest fish in the market. Her efforts did not lead to disappointment. Robert met her smile with one of his own and spoke to her as if she was a long time friend. "I have not seen you here before are you in town on business or pleasure?" inquired Tina. Robert smiled again and replied, "Both." To this, Tina asked what business brought him to L.A. and the response was nothing telling, not too revealing, simply "Sales." Robert knew what was next; it is always the same question, no matter where he was. He was prepared with his retort; it would be the same he has used over the last ten years. So when Tina asked what line of sales he was in Robert was quick to say, "Basically whatever people are looking for." This was said with that engaging smile and just a subtle hint of mischief in his eyes.

Tina was not sure what to read into what she saw but she had to admit to herself that she was intrigued. She found herself wondering who this man was. He seemed tall as he sat comfortably in the chair, his looks were ruggedly handsome and his smile was comfortable to see. Tina found herself feeling a bit unsure of herself and this was something she had not felt in many years. Granted, she was only twenty-three but she seemed to always know how to handle people. She thought of herself a good judge of character but this man was different. Feeling intrigued was exciting and she wanted to know more. Unsure of how to dig into this she simply said, "Your Crown and Coke will be $5.25." Robert smiled and pulled his money clip out of his inside coat pocket and pealed one $100 bill off and handed it to her saying, "I hope you can break this so early in the evening". Tina was impressed. Not by the bill, she saw those all the time, but by what she figured had to be a couple of thousand dollars remaining on the money clip. She gave her best charming smile and said, "I am sure the bartender could handle the bill and if not she would find the manager and make sure it was taken care of". To this Robert held up his hand and asked this cute young thing to hold on to it and that way he would not have to pay each time he had his drink refreshed. This was something new to Tina. It was an unusual request but as she thought about it, she felt pleased that this stranger seemed to trust her. With that thought running through her mind she smiled again and said she would be happy to take care of Robert's wishes.

Now seemed to be a great time to introduce herself so she offered her hand and volunteered her name. "My name is Tina and I'll be taking care of you this evening." Robert took your hand and softly squeezed and said, "Nice to meet you Tina, I am Robert and I will be glad to have you take care of me and I will take care of you as I leave." With that out of the way Robert truly wished Tina would leave so he could return to scoping out the people that were starting to come in. After a few moments, Tina excused herself and now it was back to work.

THE FINAL SCORE

Robert had been doing this for so long he had forgotten what life was like without the thrill. As he pondered this, he had to admit to himself that he really doubted he could live any other way. The money was great. By his last conversation with his banker in Aruba, he had amassed a fortune in excess of one hundred million dollars US. Money was no longer the driving force no it was the thrill. How many people could liberate that much money from so many people and live to tell. He was a con artist, an artist that everyone liked and some of his marks were so deep under his web of lies that they found themselves actually feeling sorry that he too hand been ripped off. His story was always the same. If you need to make a few hundred thousand dollars in a short period of time, Robert was the man who could assist you in doing so. He knew people who would be more than happy to sell a kilo or two of pure cocaine. So pure that it could be stepped on at least two times which would bring the street value up to at least two hundred and fifty thousand dollars. The only thing you would need to do is supply the money to make the purchase. The one thing you would never know was that there was no cocaine, never has been and never will be. Robert was too smart for that. Hell, he was an all-state basketball player in high school and had never done any drugs, at least nothing more than alcohol, nicotine, and the occasional Tylenol. No Robert sold dreams, solutions to problems; some would go as fare as to say hope. Where did this guy, from small town USA, come up with the bait to accomplish what he had?

The answer to that question is really quite remarkable. Robert was a born in the wool, die hard Democrat. Hell, he was almost a socialist; he believed that there were so many people who could not take care of their basic needs he felt the government should take on the responsibility. Yet he found his inspiration from none other than President Bush. Early in 1989, President Bush announced the "War on Drugs." As Robert heard this speech, a thought began to form in his mind. If the President was going to have a war on drugs, what role could Robert play? The more he thought about it, the answer began to become more and more clear. In his mind, Robert figured the best way to slow the spread of drugs in the US was to reduce the amount of money drug dealers had. The only problem was he knew no drug dealers and really was not to sure how to go about finding one. He was twenty-eight years old, had graduated high school and really did not know too much about the real world. However, he figured if he could hunt and trap coons for a living he could hunt and trap a few drug dealers. Therefore, with a plan in place, Robert left the small town in the Midwest and headed to St. Louis.

With less than one hundred dollars to his name Robert sat in a downtown bar in St. Louis. Not wanting to spend any money, he was drinking water with a lemon in a rocks glass. He was proud of himself because even to him it looked like vodka and soda; he just hoped others would think the same. He had to be careful and drink it slow just as if it were a vodka and soda. The last thing he wanted was someone to realize that he did not belong. As he sat at the bar, he listened to every conversation within earshot. Finally, he heard the sentence he was waiting for. One of the waitresses was talking with a regular and told the guy that she had not been able to hook up with her dealer so she did not have any coke for sale right now. She went on to say that she hoped to catch the dude during the evening so make sure to check back around midnight. The guy said he would and finished his beer and left. Robert watched to make sure the guy was leaving and got up from the bar and sat at the newly vacated table. He had drink in hand when the waitress came by to check on him so there was just some small talk between the two. Finally Robert felt that Susie was at ease and he went for the kill. In a low-level voice, he told her he had overheard her conversation about not having any product to move and maybe he could help her out. Susie was not at comfortable with this situation, she had never seen this person before and for all she knew he was a cop. Robert could sense her hesitation and did not want the opportunity to die on the vine. He reached into his pocket and pulled out the gram of coke he had purchased earlier in the day and reached for Susie's hand. He told her to try his stuff and if she liked it maybe they could work something out. Still unsure but knowing her regular customers, as she called them, would be coming in for their weekend high and she knew if she could not supply them they would go elsewhere and may not come back to her. With that thought making sense, she figured she could take a chance. She put the coke in her apron and headed for the ladies room. Robert sat there hoping that what the old friend he ran into and got the coke from had told him was true. Pat had said that his stuff was real good and he assured Robert that he would enjoy the high. Based on that information and the fact that Pat would sell it to him for only fifty bucks Robert threw caution to the wind and made the deal.

Now Robert sat and tried to figure out his next move. He knew nothing of the drug business, the only thing he knew was that Pat had told him most grams sell for around a hundred bucks and something called an eight ball went for $250. He had no idea what an eight ball was but did not want to appear stupid so he did not ask. He would later find out that this was street slang for two and half grams, hell he would learn everything about the drug business in the next few months but right now, he was flying by the seat of his pants with Susie. Staring at his glass of water, with his mind racing around blankness he did not see Susie approaching. When she spoke, he jumped as if he had heard a gunshot. She laughed at the fact that she had surprised the piss out of this guy and her laughter did not put Robert at ease. He looked up at her and did his best not to show his anger. After collecting his thoughts he smiled and asked if she liked the coke. Her answer was as plain as the smile on her face. She went as far as to say she had not had any that good in quite some time. With that being said, she asked the question that Robert was hoping she would ask, "How much could he get for her?" Robert thought for a moment and asked how much she needed and what she normally paid. Susie thought for a little and then asked if he could hook her up with an ounce. Robert said he could and again asked how much she would pay. With no hesitation Susie said she could go twenty five hundred. Robert's heart jumped in his chest as if he had just won the lottery. Now all he had to do was figure out how to get the cash out of her and get the hell out of the bar. He thought for a moment and then hatched his plan. He told her all she needed to do was come up with to money, give it to him; he would leave and have his partner come in within thirty minutes with the ounce. He went on to tell her he never let the product and the money be together as that way the deal was less conspicuous and therefore drew the least amount of attention. Susie had to think about this. She did not know this clown, why would she hand over twenty five hundred dollars to him. Damn, it would be so easy for him to just rip her off; as this was going through her mind, she heard her name called out from across the room. As she looked to see who was calling her she realized that four of her regulars where in. These guys always bought eight balls, that was a grand in her pocket. No way was she going to take a chance on loosing out on that kinda cash. She told Robert to wait and she headed over to the table were the guys were at. She was right. They were looking for her to hook them up. She asked them if they could wait for about forty-five minutes as she was waiting for her supplier to show up. She even offered to buy their first round of drinks for the inconvenience. With the idea of a free drink and some good coke, they agreed and asked for four top shelf bourbons. She thought she should have seen that coming but what the hell, a grand is still a grand. She was willing to invest twenty-five dollars to make a grand. Hell, if she played it right she would have the clown pay for the drinks.

After taking the four guys their drinks, she headed back to the stranger. She expressed her concerns to which Robert said he understood. In an attempt to ease her mind he gave her his cell phone number so that she could call him at anytime, even at some point in the future for another deal. He explained that he had just got into town and had not gotten a room yet or he would give her that information also. It took only a short period of time for Susie to give Robert an envelope full of cash. She asked him to describe his partner so she would know whom to be looking for and Robert was more than happy to do so. Robert described his fictional partner named Jamie with such detail that there could only be one man who would fit the description. With that being done, Robert got up to leave and told Susie that within the next thirty minutes all would be good. She asked him to pay for the drinks for her regulars and Robert just laughed, he told her he was not in the habit of taking care of other people's messes.

Robert got in his truck, not believing his luck and just a little bit proud of himself. The entire process had taken less than an hour. Not bad work, twenty five hundred dollars in less than an hour. Robert figured he could get real used to this new line of work. He drove downtown found the Sheraton Hotel, across from Busch Stadium, got a room and went to the bar. He had left Susie thirty-five minutes ago and knew she would be calling soon. He gave this fact much thought. He had no idea what he was going to tell her. As he sat there in the hotel bar, drinking a real vodka and soda, he overheard two men talking about a friend's son who had been arrested over the weekend for possession of drugs. It seemed that he was out on the town when a fight had broken out in the bar he was at. He was trying to leave as the police showed up and he was told to sit down. He must have said something out of line as he soon found himself in the back of a squad car and it did not take the cops long to find the small bag of grass in his back pocket. Robert found himself thinking that that kid must be really stupid but his fuck up would be Roberts out. Just then, his cell phone rang.

Robert told Susie not to be concerned that Jamie was on his way and should be there anytime. He did his best to sound casual, unconcerned, and hoped that Susie would relax and just wait. He talked with her for a few minutes and then told her if Jamie had not gotten there within the next fifteen minutes to give him a call and he was sure he would know what was going on. Susie seemed to relax and said she would wait but if he were not there soon there would be problems. Robert tried his best to remain calm and told her he was sure there was nothing to worry about. As he hung up to phone he wondered what Susie meant by "problems." The more he thought about it he realized that that was just some kind of blank threat and he really had nothing to worry about. Susie knew nothing of who he was; she had no clue as to where he was from let alone where he would be staying. She was pissing in the wind and all she was going to get was a little wet. He actually got a chuckle the more he thought about it.

Just as Robert got his second drink, his cell rang again. This time he let in ring several times before answering. Just as he figured, Susie was pissed. She wanted to know what the hell was going on. She demanded that Robert get his butt back over to her bar and he had better have the coke with him, her money, or else he was dead. Robert just listened to her screaming and cussing when she finally stopped he tried to assure her that he would find out what was going on. He went on to tell her nothing like this had ever happened before and he was sure that everything would be all right. He told her that he would make sure she was taken care of and there was no reason to be talking about anybody being killed. With that, he hung up the phone and turned it off. He did not want to be bothered by anyone least of all Susie.

Somewhere around midnight, Robert made his way to his room. He had had a very good day. He had picked up twenty five hundred dollars, had enjoyed several good drinks, had eaten a steak that was damn good, and now he was going to get a good night sleep in a comfortable bed. Anything was better than sleeping in his truck. He would talk with Suzie after he got up and would tell her about Jamie being in jail. The coke and the money were gone. There was nothing he could do. It was not his fault. They both were losers in this situation. What could he do?

At eleven in the morning the phone rang, it was Robert's wake up call. He showered and headed out to get a bite of food. He found a nice restaurant that had a champagne brunch and he ate and drank his fill. He left around one in the afternoon and decided he would take a walk around downtown. Around two he turned his phone on and it only took a couple of minutes for the first call to come in. Sure enough, it was Susie. This time she was more than pissed, she called Robert every name in the book. He thought she even used some words that he had never heard before. Deep down inside he was really enjoying this. It took everything he had not to just break out in laughter; somehow, he was able to not laugh at Susie and her problems. Each time she said she was going to have him killed he had to move the phone away from his mouth so she would not hear him chuckle. Finally, Robert got the opportunity to tell Susie about

Jamie's bad luck. He explained that he was busted while he was attempting to pick up the coke. Both he and their dealer were in jail and the bond was over one hundred thousand dollars. Robert had gotten the phone call around two in the morning and he had been up trying to arrange bond ever since, but when you do not own property, no bondsman was willing to help. This information came as a shock to Susie. She was concerned about her role in the whole thing and Robert told her that no one besides himself knew who she was; she had nothing to worry about. After a few more minutes the conversation was over. Robert, for the first time realized that he had just successfully completed his first effort in helping the President in his "War on Drugs." The smile on his face said it all.

After ten years of running the same scam, it seems hard to believe it all started with twenty five hundred dollars from some girl named Susie in St. Louis, Missouri. Since then Robert had worked all over the country. From New York, Miami, Houston, Dallas, and had made several runs to L.A. Now he was back in L.A. looking for one last desperate fool. He knew he would find the right person it would just take time. He was not concerned; he had rented a suite, a limousine, and planned to be here for at least a month. He had grown with the business and now only made deals in the high hundred thousands and sometimes even a million. He had it made, or so he thought. All he wanted was one more big score. With that completed he was through, retirement at the age of thirty-eight. All he would do is travel, play some golf, maybe get lucky and meet the right girl. He could live the life of a rock star. Money would never be a problem, hell he had enough to last a lifetime. As he sat in this upscale bar, the crowd was starting to grow. It was just as he planned, Monday Night Football would be starting in half an hour and the crowd was in an upbeat mood. All Robert had to do was sit, wait, and listen.

As the night progressed Tina made sure that Robert never had to wait on a drink. He was not paying a lot of attention to how much he had had to drink but suddenly realized that he was a bit tipsy. He became upset with himself. He had always been careful not to drink too much when he was working. He was too relaxed, had let his guard down. Now he figured

THE FINAL SCORE

the night was lost. No sense in trying to establish a relationship with someone when he may not be able to remember the stories he told. Oh but Robert did enjoy drinking. He gave it some more thought and decided what the hell. It was only Monday, he had been in town only two days and he was on no timetable. With that thought in his mind he moved to the bar. Tina came by to see if he was leaving and Robert said no he just wanted a better view of the TV, he said he realized she could no longer take care of him and to just keep the change for his first hundred. Tina smiled but felt compelled to tell this nice looking gentleman that his change was over eighty dollars. Robert simply smiled and said he guessed she was going to have a good night. Tina could not help the big smile that flashed across her perfect face; she knew this was going to be a good night.

The game between the Washington Redskins and Dallas Cowboys was just starting. The men at the bar were interested as two were from Dallas and the third one was from Washington. You could say that their interest was more than the casual fan. As they talked the conversation quickly became heated and bets were made. The bets were small but one of the men, named Billy, confessed he had placed a hundred thousand dollar bet on the Cowboys with his local bookie. He went on to say that he had to win because he did not have the money to cover if he lost. He knew he would be in a world of hurt if the Boys did not come through for him. His friends looked at him in disbelief. How in the hell does an owner from a local restaurant place that kind of bet. Billy explained that he had met the bookie early in the summer and had done very well making bets on baseball, in fact he was up about twenty grand. His biggest problem was he owed the IRS over fifty grand and with the cost of keeping his restaurant running there was no way he could cover the debt to the damn government. He was afraid that he might loose his business, his car, his house, in other words everything he had. Billy went on for some time berating the government, if one had not heard the beginning of the story it would have been easy to jump to the conclusion that this loud mouth was at a point where overthrowing the government was not a reach.

Robert just sat and smiled. He had found his mark. The only thing that was missing was the end of the game.

Now with his senses keen, Robert stopped drinking alcohol. He quietly switched to straight soda and waited for his chance to join the conversation with the three men to his left. After a while, the three became very engrossed in the game and the only things that were being said were about what was going on in Dallas. At one point there was a great play by Dallas and Robert said to Billy that things were looking up for him. Billy looked at the stranger and smiled. He quickly engaged Robert about the play and discovered he found a friend in kind, another Cowboy's fan. It did not take long before the two were reminiscing about the good-o-days involving Roger the Dodger, and all those Super Bowl victories. The greatness of Tom Landry and how Jerry Jones did him so wrong, the new owner of the Cowboys who only wanted his friend, Jimmy Johnson, to be his coach. It did not take Robert long to ask about Billy's restaurant. He discovered it was close to the Hilton, where he was staying, and Robert said he would have to come in and check out Billy's menu. Billy seemed pleased that he had meet a bird of the same flock and asked Robert to make sure he asked for him when he came in. He then extended his right hand and said, "Billy, Billy Richardson."

"Robert McGuire." Robert was more than happy to agree. As he sat back and watched the half-time discussions, he smiled to himself. He had found what he was looking for. A man with means, who had problems and of course Robert had a solution that no one else could provide. All he had to do was be patient.

As the second half began, Robert offered to buy the three a round of drinks and each seemed appreciative, none more than Billy. Billy liked the fact that someone he had just met was buying him a drink. It always seemed that Billy was the one buying drinks. Even his friends seemed to take advantage of the fact that he always had cash in his pocket. Sure, they would buy a round or two but in Billy's mind, he would be the one left with the final check. Sometimes this would piss him off but he had few friends and did not want to loose these two. It was nice to be able to hang with guys who were not in the food service business. Those clowns only discussed shop and after a while that got very old. It was nice to have a couple of friends to play golf with, to make a quick trip to Vegas with and not to have to hear about problems with vendors and staff. Billy looked forward to getting to know Robert. He seemed like a real nice guy, hell he was even a Cowboys fan.

As the game ended, it was clear that Billy was in trouble, the final score was Washington 33, Dallas 31. He had just lost one hundred thousand dollars that he did not have. The look in his eyes was one of total despair. He actually looked as if he was going to breakdown right there in the bar. The post game wrap-up had just begun when Billy's cell phone rang. He looked at the caller ID and began to visibly to shake. His two buddies stood by, not knowing what to say or do. As he answered the phone, he heard the voice of his bookie saying that he would need to collect on the bet as he had other bets he needed to cover. Billy said he understood and told the voice on the phone he could expect payment by the weekend. The bookie really did not want to hear that but realized that he needed to give this guy a little time to come up with the cash. He agreed to Billy's request but made sure that Billy understood that the weekend better not turn into a disappointment for him. Billy said he understood and quickly ended the conversation. As Billy sat on the barstool all the blood slowly disappeared from his face. His friends tried to console him but their efforts fell on deaf ears. Billy had no idea what he was going to do and said so. His new friend seemed truly concerned. Robert listened intently and did not offer any type of advice and best of all made no comment in reference to the fact that Billy should have never made that large of a bet. Wow, it was nice to meet someone new. Robert again told Billy to be careful and stood up to leave.

After he shook everyone hands he laid a hundred dollar bill on the bar and told the three that the last drinks were on him. Again they seemed appreciative but no one more than Billy. He gave Robert a little hug and thanked him again. Robert did the best he could to hide the fact that this hug made him uncomfortable and he told Billy not to worry about it, he enjoyed seeing other people happy. He then told Billy he would try to come by the restaurant for lunch on Tuesday and Billy smiled for the first time in a while. He said he was looking forward to seeing him again, and with that Robert was gone.

Back at the Hilton Robert found himself in the bar enjoying a nice glass of wine. He seemed pleased with the turn of events the night had brought. He had found the right person, with the right problems and he believed the means to allow Robert the opportunity to help him resolve the bind he found himself in. Things could not have gone better. Now all he had to do was make sure he found the restaurant for a late lunch. He figured that if it were a late lunch Billy would be able to sit with him for a while. All he needed was about ten to fifteen minutes to launch his plan to get Billy out of debt. He knew he had to be careful, Billy was a businessman and his gut instincts would tell him to be careful. Robert knew he would have to draw upon all of his experience to pull this one off. He recognized that this one could go bad, real bad real fast. He would have to go slow, take his time and make sure he had Billy right where he needed to have him. He looked down at his Rolex, it was only nine-thirty but he needed to call it a night. Robert wanted to be refreshed tomorrow and he was still suffering a little from jet lag. No matter how many times he flew from east coast to west coast he never got used to the time change. He would order another glass of wine and take it up to his suite. It was time to get some sleep. The last thing Robert did was call for a wake up call, when asked what time he thought for a moment and replied, "How about ten thirty" and with that the phone went dead.

The phone ringing brought Robert back to the conscious world. After answering the wake up call, Robert reached for the remote and out of habit turned the television on to *Fox News*. Rubbing the sleep from his eyes, he could not believe what he was seeing on the tube. It seemed that there was a major problem in New York City. He was not sure but it appeared that one of the World Trade Center towers was on fire. He quickly turned the volume up and heard that airplanes had hit both of the towers. The reporter went on to say that the planes were hijacked commercial airliners and another plane had crashed into the Pentagon and yet another had crashed somewhere in Pennsylvania. He sat there in bed in total disbelief. Watching the events unfold on the screen was totally surreal. Robert sat and wondered why this had happened, who was responsible, and what would be the response to these attacks. He soon learned that all air travel within the US had been canceled and no one knew when it would resume. The shock of today's events was slowing wearing off when Robert realized that these events would have a profound effect on his life and what he was trying to accomplish on the left coast. Just what that impact would be was yet to be realized but an impact nonetheless.

What seemed like a short period of time turned into much more. Robert turned away from the TV and realized that several hours had gone by. With that fact being understood, Robert realized that he had to get moving. He needed to shower, catch up with his limo driver and find

Billy's restaurant. Man with everything going on in New York, Robert really did not feel like going out today, he really just wished to stay in his room and continue to watch the news. He really was unsure of what to do. He wondered what if any effect today's events would have on the real business world around the country. Was Billy even open; was his limo available, what the hell was going on? Robert could not pull himself away from the news. No matter how much he tried, he was totally engrossed in what was occurring in New York, much like the rest of the country he surmised. Somewhere around two-thirty in the afternoon Robert realized that today was lost. He called down to room service and ordered a sandwich, bottle of vodka and soda, and an extra bucket of ice. Might as well be comfortable he rationalized. Within half an hour the food and drink had arrived and Robert settled in for the rest of the day. Maybe he would go out sometime in the evening, maybe not. As he looked at the clock one more time the digital numbers showed 4:00, Robert understood that the day was lost and the only thing left to do was sleep and plan on going to work on Wednesday September 12.

When the wake up call came at ten in the morning Robert woke refreshed and looking forward to what the day would bring. Again he turned the television on to *Fox News* and of course the dominate story was yesterdays events in New York. Robert realized that this was to be expected but after watching nothing but news all day yesterday he vowed that today would be different. He rose from bed, called the limo service to make sure his car and driver would be downstairs in an hour and headed for the shower. As he was getting dressed, he opened the curtains and smile at the beautiful southern California day. He loved this part of the country and if it were not for earthquakes he might even live out here. Robert reached the elevator at eleven fifteen and hoped his car was ready. As he walked out of the front doors there was the stretch Cadillac with Jose waiting to open the passenger rear door. Robert smiled; having money was nice he thought. Stopping before he got into the car, he asked Jose if he was familiar with a restaurant called The Eatery, to which Jose responded in the affirmative. Jose said, "Mr. Robert that is a very nice place and it is only a few miles from here, is that our destination?" Robert said it was but he did not want to arrive for a few hours and asked Jose to simply drive around for a while. As he stepped into the car he called up to Jose and said he decided to go to Rodeo Drive instead of driving around, he figured he would rather walk the famous street than just waste time.

Robert always enjoyed Rodeo Drive. He especially liked the people. The girls were so nice to look at and some of the men where absolute nuts. He could never quite figure out what they were trying to say with the clothes that they wore but he could always understand the girls. Oh the people of L.A., the sights one sees in this metropolitan city were distinguished to only L.A. Robert really did enjoy the people, where else could one see the things that one could see out here. Stepping into Tiffany's Robert was met with a familiar greeting by one of the sales girls. She knew him by name and by what he liked to see and sometimes buy. The two talked for sometime and the conversation was dominated by the terrorist attacks in New York. The young lady seemed worried about what was going to happen next and was L.A. on the target list. Robert did his best to try to sooth her concerns but he was unsure whether his efforts were received. Deciding that there was really nothing he was interested in, this was a surprise to the normal big spender, Robert said goodbye with certain sadness in his heart. Looking at the time, he went back to the limo and told Jose that it was time to go the restaurant.

The Eatery was a step up from what Robert expected. The white tablecloths, fine china, and the elegant wine glasses were impressive. The hostess asked if Robert was by himself today or would there be another joining him. Robert was surprised by her accent, he guess Australian, or New Zealand. Upon asking he learned she was from Sydney and had been in the states for about six months. After pleasantries, Robert let her know that he was alone and preferred a table in the rear of the smoking section. Audrey smiled and simply said, "Please follow me." Upon reaching the table Robert asked Audrey to please tell Billy that Robert was here and would very much like him to stop by when he had a minute. With that, Robert picked up the menu and started to see what he might have for this late lunch. After a few minutes a distinguished young man approached the table, introduced himself as James, and said he would be serving Robert today. He asked if Robert cared for a cocktail, glass of wine, or anything else to drink before ordering. Robert asked for a glass of Kendal Jackson Chardonnay and James smiled and left the table. As Robert's attention returned to the menu a familiar voice said hello and asked if any decision had yet been made. Robert looked up and smiled as Billy was reaching for a chair. The two shook hands and before anything else Billy asked Robert if he liked Calamari. Robert said he did and when James returned with the glass of wine Billy told him to bring out an order of Calamari. Turning his attention back to Robert, Billy asked what he thought about the events in New York. The two sat and discussed the events of yesterday in great detail. They related to each other where they were when they first learned about the attacks and how they responded to the news. It was surprising to each that the feelings they experienced were shared with the other. Billy's first thought was that Robert might have more in common with him than simply the Dallas Cowboys. He was starting to view Robert as a kind of kindred spirit, maybe someone who would become a true friend. This was exactly what Robert had hoped for, things could not be going better. Maybe even the terrorist attacks could be used as an advantage.

    James showed up with a platter of Calamari that was accompanied with some Marinara sauce that smelled as if Grandma Mia was in the kitchen. With the first bite Robert knew that Billy knew what he was doing. It was obvious to any person who eats out as much as Robert does that this man found his true calling. From what Robert had learned Monday night, his calling certainly was not accounting or gambling. This thought brought a smile to Roberts face. Billy saw the smile as a complement pertaining to the Calamari and he really felt at ease. When the Calamari was about half-gone Billy asked Robert what he would like for his main course. Robert thought for a moment and asked what the best cut of meat on the menu was. Billy smiled and said that he had the best fillet on the west coast and highly recommended it. He went on to say that they were serving this today with new potatoes, mushroom caps, and freshly steamed asparagus. Robert said that that sounded delightful and asked the steak to be cooked rare. The next time James came to the table Billy told him what Robert wanted and asked the waiter to bring another glass of wine. The conversation quickly returned to the events of yesterday. Billy freely admitted that all he could do was drink, and drink a lot. Robert smiled and said he had done the same. To Robert it seemed that most people were as transfixed as he was, in a way this was comforting and at the same time disconcerting. To experience the same feelings with so many people was new to Robert. After giving that thought some time to really digest he realized that most people, even Billy, felt the same way. Could he use this to his advantage, Robert was unsure, but he made a mental note of that and would spend some time thinking about just that. Billy excused himself saying there were a few things he needed to check on but would be back. Robert shook Billy's hand saying he understood but that he truly hoped Billy would return as there were a few things he would like to discuss. Billy agreed and on parting expressed his desire for Robert to enjoy his lunch.

Just as Robert was finishing his lunch he saw Billy headed in his direction. Billy inquired as to the level of Robert's satisfaction and was pleased to see the large smile on Robert's face. He really did not listen to the complimentary words that Robert spoke, the smile had answered his question better than any words could. After a few minutes, Billy was called away, but his thoughts were on himself. Billy did enjoy owning a restaurant and seeing the happiness that his food created for his guest. It was one of the reasons he choose to risk everything he had by opening his place. He knew the hours would be longer than anything he was use to but figured it would be worth it. Billy had opened The Eatery ten years ago; in the beginning the times were lean to say the least. By the third year Billy saw his first profit. When his accountant called to tell his client that he had made a little over seventy five thousand dollars last year and the relief that Billy felt was unimagined. For the first time he honestly believed that he could make it in this dog eat dog business. Then in the forth year the

Times finally sent out its food critic. This visit was unannounced and it was a few days later that Billy received a call from the Times telling him that they were going to run an article about the Eatery and asked if they could send a reporter by for an interview. Billy readily agreed and set up a time in the early afternoon on the next day. The interview had gone well and Billy could not wait until the Sunday edition was delivered to his home. When the day finally arrived, Billy could not believe his luck. The critic ranted and raved about the décor of the Eatery, the swiftness of service, the quality of the food, and his last remarks were nothing but outstanding about the wines available to be enjoyed. Billy rushed to the restaurant to enjoy the written word with his staff. The mood was up beat and would continue for weeks on end. Soon after the article was published Billy started to see more and more people in the restaurant, the wait list was longer and was now occurring on Mondays and Tuesdays. Things could not be better. Billy thought that he was on his way, and he was. The day he knew he had arrived was the day that Clint Eastwood was in for dinner. Billy's hope was soon realized, The Eatery was rapidly becoming the hot spot for the stars and the pictures of them entering and leaving were great for business. It was soon that Billy was clearing in excess of five hundred thousand dollars each year. He no longer was worried about money, he felt like the weight of the world had been lifted off his shoulders.

Not to bad for a guy who grew up in the housing projects of East L.A. The only downside was both of his parents had died before they saw his success. Billy missed them greatly as they were the true inspiration for his life. He had grown up watching both his mom and dad working two jobs just to keep food on the table. He remembered when he first opened The Eatery, the hours he kept were unreal but he always said that if his old man could work as hard as he did, then surely he could also. The only downer was his stupid accountant. Why was this guy so worried about how Billy paid himself? After all, it was his money, he earned it, and he was the one who had risked it all for the opportunity to be able to take a few bucks from the safe before he went out. Who was this guy who kept saying he should not do things like that? Hell, Billy was paying him damn good money to keep his books and do his taxes. In Billy's mind this spoilsport worked for him and needed to get off his ass. Now as he thought about this he wished he would have listened. How was a high school dropout supposed to know about tax laws and forms? Hell he was doing his best to make sure no checks bounced. And for his ignorance now the IRS was breathing down his neck like a grizzly bear in the great outdoors. He had tried to outrun them but much like the bear they were, that was impossible. He had just learned last week that he owed over fifty thousand dollars in back taxes and penalties and if he could not pay, he would loose The Eatery. He could also loose his car 2001 Cadillac Fleetwood damn he loved that vehicle. He could also loose his home. Man the damn government was too big and too mean. He had to find a way to get this bill paid. His banker had listened with true interest but told him due to the other loans that Billy had outstanding there was no way the bank could help him. What the hell was he going to do?

When Billy met John David, the bookie, he thought maybe he had found his answer. He set up an account with JD so that he could make bets over the phone. And did he make bets. What had started out as a little fun soon became an obsession. Billy had always loved sports and believed he knew more than the casual fan. He turned his knowledge of baseball into some easy cash. After he won his first ten bets, he decided it was time to parlay his luck and smarts into some real winnings. By the first of September he had built his account up to roughly twenty thousand dollars. JD liked the fact that his newest client was not always hounding him to collect his winnings. This guy, Billy, seemed more interested in placing more bets than collecting his winnings. For that reason when Billy said he wanted to place a bet on the upcoming Monday Night Football game for one hundred thousand dollars he only had to think about it for a day or two. JD knew he could cover the bet if he lost but was more interested in how winning would change his life. It did not take long for his to accept this bet. JD figured that he could parlay the winnings into several times that amount because he would finally be able to accept larger bets from his customers. Hell, he might even try to figure out how to advertise his services. He had heard of some bookies who did advertise on the internet. When he collected his winnings he would have to investigate this idea.

Returning to the smoking section, Billy sat down at the table being occupied by his newest friend, Robert, the only true thought on his mind was his money problems. How was he going to deal with the IRS and now his bookie? He was more concerned about the IRS, maybe that was just plain stupidity, and he really was not sure. Robert could sense that the man who just sat down was in deep thought. He wondered if now was the time to brooch the subject and decided that he probably should wait. He would let Billy bring up the debt he incurred last night at the hands of the Cowboys. It did not take long. After again asking about the meal, Billy once again thanked Robert for buying the drinks for him and his friends. Robert smiled and said it was the least he could do for someone who had had the night that Billy had had. He made sure to emphasized the least he could do part, hoping that Billy would take the bait. At first, it appeared that the statement had gone cleanly over the head of the expected target. Billy showed no response, he seemed only interested in making sure Robert understood his true appreciation for the drinks that were bought. Robert figured he would just go with the flow because he knew better than to attempt to move too fast. The last thing he wanted to do was scare this guy off. He felt he had read the guy correctly, yes he had money problems, that was a given. Yes, he appeared to have the means that would make it worth Robert's time to work him as only he could. He just needed to pick the right time to bring Billy inside, where Robert wanted him to be. Robert stated that he was glad that Billy enjoyed and appreciated what he had done and would not mind doing it again, maybe tonight. Billy smiled but said he was not sure, he had to admit that he had overdone it a bit last night. Still licking my wounds from Monday night and with the events of yesterday, I had to go out last night; guess I over did it again. When pushed he admitted that he had trouble making it in this morning. This was something that was not usual for Billy. He went on to say that, he had been with both of the guys he was with Monday night and they too had the same problem this morning. To this, Robert had to laugh aloud. He found this to be very funny, he was even a little jealous because he had not left the suite. He then said, "if not tonight maybe Thursday night, besides I think most people could use a little time away from all the bad news on the television." Billy shook his head in agreement and stated, "That for him Thursday would be better." Robert pondered about this, thinking that this would not fit into the time frame of the bookie. Not knowing quite how to address this concern Robert decided to let it go. He figured if this clown was not overly concerned then he certainly should not be either. Billy then admitted that he was in such bad shape last night he had to call a cab as opposed to tempting fate and getting a DWI. The worst part was he then had to catch a cab to the restaurant this morning.

Robert smiled at this; he remembered the last time he made the same decision. He saw an opening and did not want it to get away. Upon wondering where his server was, Billy told him not to worry lunch was on him. Robert thanked him, pulled a twenty out of his pocket, and asked that Billy would make sure James got his tip. With that the two shook hands and agreed to get together soon for those drinks.

Before he left he told Billy he could give him a ride to the bar to get his car if he would like. Billy smiled at hearing this, as he really did not want to have to ask one of his staff members for a ride. He would rather them not know that the boss had tied one on last night. He agreed to take Robert up on his offer and the two made their way towards the front door. Stepping outside the sun made both men squint against its brightness. It took a few seconds before they could see and Billy asked where Robert had parked. He motioned towards the limo, and as they got closer, Jose stepped out and opened the rear door. As Robert approached, he told Jose that they needed to return to the same bar as Monday night. Billy was surprised by the events that were playing out in front of him. He had thought that Robert had some money but did not think that this guy was the limo type. Getting into the car he said something about it must be nice, to which Robert said, "It sure but it beat the hell out of trying to drive in this town." Billy had to agree that not being from here this alternative probably was better than a rental car. As they reached the bar, Robert gave Billy his cell phone number and room number at the Hilton so he would be able to get in touch with him about getting together for a few drinks.

After Billy got out of the car, Jose asked where Robert wanted to go. It was late in the afternoon and with the events in New York, Robert was unsure as to where to go or what to do. He knew he did not want to return to the Hilton for if he did he would just sit in his room and watch the television. He guessed that the only thing that would be on was news pertaining to the attacks and honestly he had had his fill already. There was nothing that he could do and thank God no one close to him was involved. The last thing he wanted to do was sit in a hotel room and watch the twin towers burn, and fall over and over again. He had seen it several times yesterday and really had no desire to see it again. He told Jose to just drive; he did not care where but to just drive. With that being said, Jose headed for the interstate.

After driving around for a couple of hours Robert asked Jose if he new of any other bar near the Hilton. Jose said he was sure there were a few but the one he was at Monday night was the nicest. Based on that, Robert told Jose to drop him of there, and upon arrival, he told Jose that he could leave. He said he would call the service when he was ready to leave but it may be several hours. Jose agreed and wished his client a good time. Robert smiled and told Jose he would see him later.

Walking towards the door he glanced at his watch, the time was 5:30. Perfect Robert thought, just in time for happy hour. As he stepped inside The Varsity, the first person he saw was Tina. He was happy that she was working again tonight and he hoped she would be taking care of him. To his surprise, Tina saw him, came up, and asked how he was doing. Robert replied that he was better and asked her to take him to a table that she could take care of him. This brought a smile to her face, man what a face, what a smile Robert thought. She walked him towards a table in the front of the bar to which Robert asked if he could sit more towards the back.

Tina said sure and walked towards a table more towards the rear to the place. As Robert sat down, Tina asked if he was going to enjoy another Crown and Coke or if he had another pleasure he wished for. This brought a smile to Robert, as he was impressed that she remembered what he drank. He simply said that would be fine and watched her walk away as he lit a cigarette. He had to be honest the walk was nice. Now he began to wonder what this young lady was like. Was she a student? Was she hopping for the first acting job to come along? Where was she from? He figured if given the opportunity he would find out answers to those questions and all the others that were racing around his head. Robert was glad that the bar did not appear to busy and he hoped Tina would have the time to have a conversation with him.

As Tina turned in her order, she asked Mike, the bartender, to make it a good one. She really wanted to make this man happy. After all, he had given her what had amounted to a little more than eighty-dollar tip on just three drinks Monday night. Moreover, he was right when he said he thought that she was going to have a good night, which was an understatement to say the least. She had actually made over two hundred dollars in six hours on a Monday night. That was damn good and she wanted to show her appreciation as best she could. When she brought Robert his drink she asked him to taste it as she had requested the bartender to make it a good one. Smiling Robert brought the glass to his mouth and took the first sip. It was strong, stronger than the other night but he had to admit, it was good. This information brought that amazing smile to Tina's face, this pleased Robert to no end.

He asked if Tina had a few minutes to talk and she told him that on this night if things do not get busier that might be all she could do. With that, the two started asking each other questions as fast as they could. Robert learned that Tina was from Vancouver, British Colombia and had been in L.A. a little over a year. No she was not here trying to become an actress. She laughed at that question but had to admit she may be the only girl in town that was not taking acting lessons. She told Robert that she had her degree in computer graphics and was trying to get her own business going. When asked, she had to admit that she had done a few things but not enough to pay the rent. Most of what she had done was covers for CD's by upstart bands and occasionally for a new business owner who either could not manipulate a computer or afford one of the larger advertising firms. She hoped that one day one of the bands makes it big or enough people talked about her work that she could get enough projects going that she could get out of the waitress gig.

Listening to this beauty was relaxing, and Robert really enjoyed the conversation. He also liked the fact that she did not ask too many questions about him and what he did. He figured that he liked this place and probably would continue to come in and did not want to have to remember the stories he told her. However, he had to be honest with himself he really liked Tina. This was unusual for Robert. He had learned many years ago to keep his guard up and keep people at arms length at best. It was easier not get to know someone, especially since he probably would not see them again. Yeah it made life somewhat lonely but if he wanted he could always hire a wife for the night. He liked that part of his life, no commitments, no hassles, no worries, and most important no questions. The last part of that thought was the most important. That was the main reason he had not had a girlfriend over the last ten years, no questions. It was indeed lonely but at least his personal life was not complicated. Somehow, this young lady had sparked something within him. The spark was enough that he wanted to investigate where it came from. While these thoughts were going through his mind Tina had been telling him about growing up in Vancouver. He did the best job he could to act as if he was listening but he was really hoping that she would not ask any questions about what she had said.

Much to his relief Tina said she needed to go see what her manager wanted. Robert said that he understood and asked her if she would bring him another drink when she had a minute. He smiled as she turned to leave. The smile was for her to see and because he was happy that he was going to see that walk again. Damn it sure was nice. As he sat there, he looked around the bar and realized that he had made the correct decision to come in Monday night because there were no more than three or four tables occupied and only two people at the bar. Hell, this was slow, especially for L.A. He was glad that the jet lag that had bothered him was not too bad as Monday night proved valuable. He looked up to see Tina returning with his drink and she had an unusual smile on her face. Unusual because he had not seen it before, it seemed to have a hint of mischief in it. As she set the drink down and picked up the empty, she looked directly into his eyes and said, "I am off!" This took Robert by surprise and he did a bad job of hiding his disappointment. Tina noticed this and made a funny sound as she pushed his hair back from his forehead. As he looked back in her eyes, she asked if it would be ok for her to join him for a drink. This brought the smile back to Roberts face and he said, "Sure as long as she would not get into any kind of trouble." She replied that she had already cleared it with her boss, she had told him Robert was an old friend from Vancouver and she just wanted to spend some time with him. She then said she needed to go change out of her uniform and asked if Robert would wait. He said he certainly would and then handed her a twenty to pay for his first two drinks. She smiled and said she would be right back.

What was the longest five minutes of his life, Robert was truly happy to see Tina emerge from the back. Damn she looked good. Dressed in a short black skirt with a white top that appeared to be more like a blouse than a pullover. She also wore a pair of black and white high heels that really set the outfit off. As she approached the table, she again flashed that smile that had found its way through Roberts's defenses. He did not mind at all, in fact he was glad that they had met. As she sat down Robert asked if she wanted something to drink and she said, "Absolutely." She turned and flagged down one of the waitresses and ordered a Crown and Coke. Robert wondered if this was for his benefit of if she normally drank Crown. What the hell he thought, so he just asked. The question brought laughter from Tina and she asked if he thought she was that superficial. Did he really think that she would order something just because he was drinking the same? She went on to say that she enjoyed either Crown or a nice glass of wine. Unfortunately, this bar did not stock any wine that she liked so Crown it was. After a few drinks, the conversation and laughter were completely normal. If anyone were curious, they would have thought that these two had known each other for years. Robert realized how comfortable he felt and hoped that Tina felt the same. He wanted to ask, but decided to let that go, it was not like him to be concerned with how someone else felt unless that person was a mark. Tina was not a mark, he did not know what she was, but he knew she was not a mark and he liked that. Robert glanced at his watch and realized that the two had been talking for about forty-five minutes. Damn, time did fly by when you were having fun. He really did not want this to end. About that time Tina asked if he wanted another drink and Robert replied by asking, "Would you rather have dinner?" This took Tina by surprise but she liked the idea. She said that would be nice and asked if Robert had a restaurant in mind. He had to admit to himself that he had not thought that far in advance, so he simply said, "Wherever you would like." With that being settled, Robert reached for his phone and called the car service to so they could be picked up. As he hung up, he asked Tina if she would like another drink, as it would be half an hour before his ride would be here.

Ride, Tina thought. What the hell is this guy talking about? What did he do, call a friend to come and pick him up? Now she was worried that she had made a huge mistake. How could she get out of this? She started looking around the bar, hoping to find a friendly face that could help her correct her mistake but found no one she knew. Now she had to answer his question about the drink. She felt like having another and figured what the hell, at least with another drink she might be able to figure some way out of this situation. Damn, she liked this man. Why could he not be a little more regular? At least he could have a motorcycle, which would be better than waiting for a friend to give them a ride. Why did he not have a rental car, she wondered. She felt pretty safe in assuming he could afford one. Maybe he didn't have a credit card, yeah that could be it, but why would a man who appears to be successful not have a credit card. Tina's mind was racing faster than usual, she knew she had to catch her snap; otherwise she would not be able to figure someway out of this mess. The next round of drinks came and now it was time for more small talk. She hoped that Robert had not picked up on her change in attitude and did her best to continue talking.

By time they were finishing their drinks Robert stood up and said that the car was here. Tina turned too see who this friend was but saw no one at the door. Nevertheless, she saw no way out of this mess. She stood and slowly began walking towards the door, she hoped it was not as bad as she thought. Robert opened the door for her and as she stepped out the first thing she saw was a beautiful Mercedes Benz with a man standing with the passenger door opened. The man said good evening to Robert and asked for the ladies name. Robert introduced Tina to Jose and they stepped in the car. Tina's mind now was racing faster than it had been earlier. Now she really did not know what to think. She was embarrassed because of what she had been thinking back in the bar and was also glad she had not found some way to get out of going. She turned and looked at Robert and asked the million-dollar question, "Who the hell are you?" Robert smiled and said, "I am just a guy who got lucky and picked the right bar to walk in on a Monday night." This brought that beautiful smile back to Tina's face, which made Robert happy. Now the only thing they needed to do was decide where to go for dinner.

After the two of them had settled into the back seat of the Benz, Robert looked into Tina's eyes, smiled, and asked her where she thought would be a nice place to have diner. She gave this thought and replied, "I really do not eat out very often but I have heard that a restaurant not far from here is very nice, it's called The Eatery." This brought a slight smile to Robert's face. He wondered if he should tell her that he had had lunch there, after thinking about this he decided that he should as he felt that Billy might very well stop by the table. Therefore, he simply stated, "I know that place, in fact I befriended the owner Monday night and had lunch there. I think that will be an excellent choice." Tina smiled at hearing that. With this being settled Tina asked Robert about his feelings in regards to the events that had occurred in New York yesterday. Robert spoke in terms of the callousness of the attack. He then wondered how many people had actually died. He expressed great respect for all the firefighters and police officers and wondered how many people would have run into those towers in an effort to save lives knowing full well that they more loose theirs in the process. Tina could only nod in agreement, as she was shaken by the whole situation. She told Robert that she had several friends that live and work in New York and two of them worked at the World Trade Center. She went on to say that with most of the phones out of order that she had not been able to discover if anybody had actually been involved. All she could do now was pray and hope for the best. Robert went on to say that he too knew a couple people that worked in the Twin Towers and like Tina had not been able to find out how they were. This conversation had left both of these two somewhat emotionally down and each was trying to lift themselves up. Tina reached over and laid her right hand lightly on Robert's left hand. He responded by taking her hand and giving it a slight squeeze. Tina responded in kind. Both seemed to be real comfortable with each other. Robert realized this, and was unsure just how he should proceed. He decided to just go with the flow, besides he was happy and did enjoy Tina's company.

As the car came to a stop outside The Eatery Jose stepped from the driver's seat and opened the passenger door so that Tina and Robert could exit the car with no trouble. As Robert got out of the car, Jose inquired how much time Robert thought they may need. Robert thought for a moment and smiled and had to say her was not sure. Jose said, "that that would not be a problem, he would just find a place to park and wait." Robert smiled as he reached for his money clip and handed Jose a twenty-dollar bill and told him to find somewhere to eat. He felt that Jose would have plenty of time to have a nice meal and relax for a bit. This brought a smile to Jose's face as it had been a long time since one of his clients had taken a moment to think of him. He thanked Robert for his kindness and climbed back in the limo and left, searching for someplace to escape for a while

Tina having observed this act of kindness was happy, comfortable, and relaxed. She felt that this man was a true gentleman; he was intelligent, well groomed, and dressed to the nines. Had she found the man she had been searching for, or would the other shoe drop. She expected the other shoe to drop, for that is what normally happened in her life. With these thoughts running through her mind she threw caution to the wind, reached up, and gave Robert a slight kiss. Nothing to over the top, just a little peck that brought a smile to Robert, who reached down and gave Tina a little hug and both gave the other a smile and a little laugh. With this first step being taken, they simply stepped into the open door, held by a short doorman, and requested a table for two in the smoking section.

With a bottle of wine and an order of Calamari to start the evening, conversation was coming so naturally. These two were truly interested in each other and both wanted to go slow with the dinner as neither wanted the night to end. As things were becoming deeper with each passing thought, a familiar voice interrupted the two. Billy could not contain his happiness in seeing Robert. He was also very surprised to see Tina, as he had seen many a man make their move on her, only to crash and burn. She was so good looking none could stay away, not even those who had a little lady at home. She had always been nice but had also always found a way to put each and every one of these hardlegs in their place. Robert sensed Billy's surprise and could not hold his thoughts back. He looked at Billy and said, "What's the matter my friend you look like the cat who just ate the canary, ye of little faith." Billy could only smile. In his mind he could only think, "To the victor go the spoils." At least this man, who had more problems than most was able to keep this thought to himself. No instead, he stated how happy he was to see the two of them and asked if there was anything he could do to assure their night met their expectations. Robert smiled and said he believed that everything would be just fine, as long as the food was as good as it was yesterday. Billy said he could guarantee that that would be the case and told them he would check back on them as the night went on. Shaking hands Billy left the two alone. He smiled as he walked away, he was impressed that Robert seemed to be able to accomplish something that no other had been able. Needless to say, Billy was impressed. He vowed to get to know this man much, much better.

As Tina and Robert were finishing their dinner, Billy reappeared and inquired as to how they had enjoyed their meal. Both stated that they were very pleased and complemented Billy on a job well done. Then the restaurant owner said that he had turned in an order for their dessert and had an excellent dessert wine, that he believed they would enjoy. When asked about the dessert, Billy smiled and said, "Bananas Foster." Robert then asked about the wine and Billy told him it was an Italian desert wine named Vensonto. Robert said he had heard of it but had not tried it before now, and he was looking forward to doing so. Billy told them it would be a few minutes before the food was ready and he stayed to talk. After a few minutes he finally got around to asking Robert what he had planned for tomorrow. Robert said he was open, and Billy asked if he would like to meet for a drink in the evening. Robert smiled and said he would be happy to do that, and asked Billy for a phone number to reach him. Billy said that he could be reached here at the restaurant and he would like to get together sometime around nine. Robert said that was fine and he would just stop by around that time. By now the Bananas Foster and the wine had been delivered to the table and Billy said "Enjoy" as he walked away. Both Robert and Tina took a bite of the Fosters and a sip of the wine. Both had to be honest, the wine was great but each had had better Fosters. As they sat and enjoyed the wine, each continued to ask questions of the other. It was clear that each one was trying to get to know the other as best they could. Robert had learned that Tina really had no plans for the rest of her life and Tina discovered that Robert was hoping to be able to relocate to Florence, Italy to spend the greater part of the rest of his life. This, like just about the rest of what Tina had learned, intrigued her greatly. She had yet to find out just who Robert worked for or exactly what he did. This she found unusual as most people identified themselves buy what they do. She figured that he was just hesitant to get into all of that, she really did not think he was trying to hide anything.

    Robert was doing his best job of not revealing too much about himself. He knew he had to be careful, and had to admit that this was uncharted waters. With each question, that Tina asked he would answer as quickly as he could, with a short answer, and then go back to her and her story. He was good at this. He knew how to get people to talk about themselves and also knew that most people felt that nothing was as interesting as their personal story. Tina was no different. She would answer most of his questions in what seemed to be an open and honest manner and rarely did she hesitate. Robert knew all the questions, he just had to make sure he did not sound rehearsed. He must have been doing a good job, Tina appeared completely relaxed and at ease both with his questions and his answers and especially with him.

After being at The Eatery for over two and half hours, they figured it was time to leave. Robert went and checked to make sure that Jose had returned, seeing the car parked near the door he returned to the table and collected Tina. As they were getting into the car, Jose asked how their meal was. Both simply smiled and asked about his. Jose said, "It was nice, he just wished he could have had a drink to go with it." Robert found this particularly funny and told his driver that he should have had that drink, to which Jose said his job was more important than any drink. Robert asked where Tina would like to go. Her answer caught him totally by surprise. "How about your hotel" Tina said. Robert looked at her and asked if she were sure and to this she said, "Absolutely." Robert just smiled and told Jose to take them to the Hilton.

As the two got to Robert's room there was no longer a need to talk. They sat in the living area, listening to some nice soft music and began to kiss. Both seemed interested in taking things slowly, not from being unsure, but rather from wanting to make sure each were enjoying what was happening and what lay ahead. It did not take them long to find themselves in the bedroom.

Tina opened her eyes and realized she was not in her apartment. She took a moment to look around the room and then remember she had gone back to the hotel with Robert. A smile slowly came over her face. She looked around and realized that she was alone. Glancing at the clock on the bedside table she discovered that it was 10:30am. She pulled herself out of bed, headed to the bathroom and found a nice, heavy, bathrobe. Putting it on, she walked out of the bedroom into the living area of the suite. The he was, sitting a small table drinking what appeared to be a cup of coffee. Walking up behind him, she leaned over his shoulder and after saying good morning, she gave him a nice kiss. She was happy that Robert responded in kind. As she sat down, pouring herself a cup, Robert said it was about time she woke up. He thought she might sleep the day away. To this she just laughed. Robert wanted to know if there was anything she wanted to do or if she just wanted to be lazy and hang out here in the room. The thought of spending a lazy day with the man that she was already developing feelings for sounded great but Tina knew she had to get home, if for no other reason she had to get to work by four this afternoon. She let Robert know this and she could see the disappointment in his eyes. This made her feel good and sad at the same time. Damn, why was rent due in two weeks. Not to mention all the other bills that she was behind on. Robert told her that he had already spoken to the car service and transportation would be here around noon. He figured they could get a bite of lunch and he would take her to her car. Lunch sounded good as

Tina realized she was getting hungry. She thought that they must have worked dinner off, this brought a smile to her face.

After finishing his cup of coffee, Robert said he was going to shower and get dressed. She was welcome to join him or she could wait until he was finished. He smiled as she thought about this, stood up, and made his way to the shower. After a few minutes, Tina thought what the hell and went to join him in the shower. Both were dressed by 11:30am and made their way downstairs. Robert saw the stretch Cadillac outside and made his way towards the door. As they stepped outside Jose was quick to get out from behind the wheel and open the door for them. After getting in Robert asked Jose to take them to Chinatown, he was looking for a restaurant and asked Jose if knew of a good one. Jose told him to leave it to him and all would be fine. Traffic was backed up, as usual. This is why Robert always hires a service when he is in town. Having a nice car, a good driver, and a beautiful girl just topped the day. Shortly Jose pulled the car in front of a restaurant and quickly had the door open for his two clients. He told Robert he would be right around the corner and for the two to enjoy themselves.

As Robert and Tina stepped inside they immediately knew they where in a true Chinese restaurant. The décor seemed right out of Hollywood and the staff seemed to be unable to speak much English. It did not take long for lunch to be served and the food was excellent. The service was top notch and very friendly. Robert made a mental note that he would have to remember this place, he wonder if dinner was different from lunch. He would like to find out. As Tina was finishing her meal Robert asked, "Where do you need to go, home or back to the bar to get your car?" Tina had to tell him that she had no car, the bus was her limo, and asked if a ride home would be out of the question. Robert smiled at this, he said that would be fine on one condition. "One condition, I wonder what that would be," replied Tina. To this, Robert smiled and asked, "When he could see her again." Tina said she would leave that up to him. He knew where she worked, would know where she lives, and if he wanted she would give him her cell number.

THE FINAL SCORE

As the car pulled away from the curb in front of Tina's condo Robert had to smile to himself. He did enjoy being with her and what had happened last night had been a bonus. This was all fine and dandy but it was time to get back into a work state of mind. He would be meeting with Billy tonight and he needed to develop a plan of attack. He knew he could not be too aggressive but he was not sure how slow he should play this one. He spent some time going over some of the past scams he had run and tried to find one that was at least similar. The more he tried; he realized that this seemed to be a new area. He was in deep thought as Jose attempted to find out what the plan was. Jose was a little surprised that Robert did not hear a word that he had spoken. Afraid to interrupt the man in the backseat he decided that he would just continue to drive around downtown L.A. After about fifteen minutes, Robert, looking out the window realized that they were downtown. He asked Jose if there was a mall nearby and was happy to hear that there was. He asked Jose to take him there he needed to walk around. He always thought better when he walked.

It did not take long for Jose to reach the mall and Robert was glad to get out of the car, even though the air was anything but clean. He was glad when he reached the doors of the mall, anything was better than the smog. As he walked slowly, almost aimlessly, he played the situation that Billy was in around in his head. As best as he could tell, this man was at least one hundred and fifty thousand dollars in the hole. The biggest question on Robert's mind was how much Billy would want to go for. Experience had taught Robert one big lesson, when people thought they had the chance to get their hands on fast, easy, and tax-free money, the natural human nature of greed played a big role in their decision. It never seemed to amaze Robert how people who just needed to come up with say fifty thousand dollars almost always wanted at least four times that. Of course, who was Robert to try to change their mind? All this meant was more money for Robert. Who was he to argue with that type of logic? What he needed to find out was how much Billy thought he needed and more importantly how much money he could get his hands on. Robert felt that he had little to do to get Billy to believe that he was the man who could help him. How to play this one? That was the true question that Robert needed to find the answer.

Time would be his best friend in this matter. He was in no rush; his only concern was the bookie. He would just have to deal with that, maybe he would even make himself available to discuss the debt with the bookie on Billy's behalf. Robert looked up and saw the mall clock, it read 5:00pm, it was time to head back to the Hilton and get ready for his appointment with Billy.

At 8:30, Robert went down to the lobby hoping that Jose would be waiting with the car. His hopes were answered as he saw Jose standing besides the Benz. As Robert stepped outside, he quietly told Jose that the first stop was The Eatery and he and Billy would be going for drinks from there. He also told Jose that this may be a late night but he would need to be available at a moments notice. Jose said that that would not be a problem; he would remain with the car and would be ready for whatever Robert needed.

In ten minutes, they were outside The Eatery.

Stepping in the doors Robert was pleased to see Billy at the hostess stand. When Billy looked up and saw Robert he immediately asked, "Are you ready to go or would you rather start here?" Robert gave this a minute of thought and responded, "Whatever you prefer." Billy smiled and said he just wanted to get the hell out of here. As they got into the back of the Benz, Billy started talking about how the mood in the restaurant was down. He said that the staff and most guests, the few that had come in, seemed to be in a mild case of shock. He then wondered how long this would last. Robert responded by saying he felt that most of the country was in a mild case of shock and he believed that it would take a few more days before people started coming around. He went on to say that with MLB and the NFL postponing all games and with air travel being stopped that there was so much upheaval in peoples life that until some sort of normalcy was brought back that most people would just be kinda numb.

Billy had to agree. He went on to say that, despite his best efforts, he too was having trouble dealing with the events of the past few days. Robert said he understood, he went on to state that if he did not have things to keep him occupied he too would be having the same problem. As the two continued to discuss the past couple of days, they noticed the car was coming to a stop. Billy asked where they were and Robert said he had heard of this place from one of the guys at the Hilton. He thought the name was Excalibur. Billy smiled and said he had been there a few times and really liked the place. He described the layout, dance floor on the ground floor, sports bar on the second and some kind of private bar on the third. He had never been to the third floor but had been told it was a cigar bar and supposedly had some real hot cocktail girls taking care of the high rollers. Robert smiled and told Billy, "We will just have to check out the high-rollers room. We need to find out if it truly is what people say it is." He went on to say that, the guy at the Hilton described the place just as Billy had and had offered his membership card to the private bar. This sounded great to Billy, he had always wanted to go into that area but could not justify the twenty thousand a year to gain access. Robert had to be honest, there was no way he would ever drop that kind of money, even if he could afford it, for a place to go and buy drinks. Robert showed the man at the door the membership card and they were escorted to an elevator that only went to the third floor.

As the doors opened the two men where greeted by a lovely young lady wearing a long tight black skirt with a slit almost up to her hip and a matching halter top that barely held her nice breast. They were shown to a table towards the rear of the room, Robert made a note of the fact that few of the table were occupied and wondered if this was normal or if things were slow due to the events over the past few days. As they sat down the young woman handed them a menu listing all the special bottles that the room had. It also showed a very impressive wine list and included names of cigars that would impress most who smoked on a regular basis. Robert suggested a warmed brandy and a Punch cigar. Billy seemed pleased with the suggestion and simply nodded his agreement. Before the drinks arrived, Billy began talking about the Monday Night Football game and mention how on several plays Dallas seemed uninterested in the game. Robert had to agree but asked if Billy thought they had given the game away or had they simply been out played. Billy started to rant and rave about how the Cowboys had not played well and in doing so had cost him one hundred grand. It was easy for Robert to see and hear the frustration in and on Billy's face and voice. He knew that Billy was right where he wanted him, all he had to do was play his cards correctly, and he stood to make a good wage for his efforts.

As the next two brandies arrived, the conversation had taken a turn to the unfortunate situation that Billy found himself in. Robert had asked the million-dollar question, "Have you heard from the bookie again?" Billy shook his head to signify the negative and said, "I don't think he will call until Saturday, if I am lucky." Robert smiled but was not sure what lucky would be for Billy. Billy continued to talk saying, "I really don't know what I am going to do. There is no way I can pay off that debt and never have been in this type of situation before. I don't know how to go about getting more time." He was afraid to say just how worried he was. He wondered if this was the type of guy who would carry someone or would rather just beat the hell out of him first and then lay down the ultimatum. With those thoughts running through his mind, Billy turned towards Robert, making sure he had his attention, and asked, "The other day, at my place, you said something to the effect that buying drinks Monday night was the least you could do. What did you mean by the least?" Now Robert knew he had him. How do I play this Robert thought? He sat back in his chair, pulled a long drag on the Punch, and said, "I might know a way to help you raise the kind of cash you need." This got all of Billy's attention. "What would I have to do and is it legal?" Billy asked. To this Robert responded, "What the hell do you care if it's legal, you're the one with a major cash flow problem." Billy had to agree, what did it matter if the action he took was legal or not, if he could get his hands on some cold hard cash he really did not care. He told Robert that he was right, but he still wanted to know what it was and how could he get involved. Robert again took a long draw on his cigar, picked up his glass and took a sip. Smiling, he placed the snifter back on the table and looking directly into Billy's eyes he said, "I know some people that could set you up with something that you could sale, and sale quick, to cover all of your debts and possible even more.

The thought of being able to get his hands on more than the one hundred and fifty thousand dollars that he owed, quickly got Billy's attention. There were several thoughts running through his mind but the one that stood out was drugs. It had to be drugs. What else was there that one could move quick enough that would generate that much of a return. Sure, he had done drugs when he was younger, but he had never been involved in the sale of the high. As this thought began to sink in, he began to wonder if he even could move the amount of drugs that would make the amount of money that he owed. While Billy sat and thought these thoughts Robert sat, comfortably, in his chair and watched both Billy and the beauty that was taking care of a table nearby. He remained relaxed and confident as Billy processed what little information he had received. Finally, Billy leaned forward and asked, "Are you talking about drugs?" Robert smiled and nodded his head up and down. Billy now knew what was being discussed, he sat back in his chair and tried to let this information sink in. He knew he had troubles but he was unsure if he really wanted to go down this road. Billy looked at Robert and said, "Tell me more."

Robert could hardly control his happiness that the conversation had reached this point. If experience taught him anything it was that once the mark had reached the point that he wanted to know more, usually there was no turning back. Sure there had been the few times that misjudgment had led to a person not being able to come up with the cash required to consummate the deal, but thankfully those had been few and far between. Robert was self-assured that that was not the case when it came to Billy. He had been able to determine that other than the IRS, Billy was flush with cash and his restaurant was very profitable. All he needed to do was find out how much Billy was looking to cash in on and just what he was willing to part with.

THE FINAL SCORE

Robert leaned forward, Billy did the same, and Robert spoke. "I know some people who move large quantities of cocaine throughout the country. Because of my connections with these people, sometimes they allow a buyer the chance to make a move. All it takes is the ability to get your hands on the cash required and then move the product." Billy was interested and asked, "What type of investment is required up front?" To this Robert said, "How much money do you want to make?" This question really got the wheels spinning inside Billy's mind, how much indeed. Did he simply want to pay off his debts or would having some extra cash around be nice. If he wanted some extra, how much extra would he want? Billy did not know the answer to that question. He needed time to figure it all out.

Time, how much do I really have, thought Billy, what with the bookie and the IRS breathing down his neck, Billy really had no idea. Thinking about time Billy asked, "How long does something like this take?" Robert said that depended on a few of different things. These things ranged from how fast the coke could be made available, how fast Billy could raise the cash required, and what if any impact the terrorist attacks may have on moving things around the country. The last thing that Robert said was something that Billy had not thought about. Damn, this could take some time, and time was something that he was running out of. He expressed this concern to Robert in hopes that he might have an idea that would prove to be worthy. Robert thought for a moment and said to give him some time on that, maybe he could come up with something that would help Billy out of this jam. Out of desperation Billy blurted out, "Like what!" Robert raised his hand and told Billy to just calm down and take a drink. Having Billy loose his cool was the last thing Robert wanted to have happen; however seeing the desperation that Billy was feeling was a good thing.

After a few minutes, Robert leaned over to Billy and said, "Maybe I could talk to your bookie and convince him to give you the time you need." The thought of this was welcomed to Billy. He thought that he just might have hit the jackpot when it came to meeting Robert. He could very easily become a true friend. Billy did not want to take a chance to ruin that, let alone have anything come between himself, Robert, and the deal to save his butt. "What would you say to JD on my behalf?" asked Billy. Robert smiled and honestly said right now he really had no idea, but he was going to give it a lot of thought. In the back of his mind, Robert believed that he could convince this JD guy to give Billy enough time to come up with the cash he owed. It would just take a bit of skill, the type of skill that Robert had plenty of. Yeah, he thought, I can pull this off. A smile began to appear on his face.

Robert glanced at his watch and saw it was 11:30. He got the waitress's attention and ordered one more round. The young woman asked if they would enjoy another cigar, to this Robert declined. After the next round was delivered, Robert asked Billy, "Do you think you could get JD to The Eatery either Friday or Saturday?" Billy said he felt pretty sure that he could, but why would he want to? Robert smiled and said, "So I can meet him." It was that simple. All Billy needed to do was get the guy to the restaurant, make sure Robert knew when he would be there, and leave the rest to him. Robert told Billy, "I do not know yet how I will take care of this but trust me, I will." This statement made Billy feel good, he actually started to relax for the first time since the damn football game was over.

Now it was time to find out how much his solution would cost him. Billy again leaned over towards Robert and asked, "How much will all of this cost me?" Again, Robert wanted to know how much he needed to make. Billy had no idea and said as much. Then he asked, "What is the most Robert had ever saw someone make?" Robert smiled and said, "The most I had ever seen was a little over a million, but the normal ran between half and three quarters of a million. It really depended on the initial investment." Billy gave this some thought and finally offered that he felt like he could get his hands on something like seventy-five thousand and wondered what that could be turned in to. Robert calmly said that he could expect somewhere between three hundred and five hundred thousand dollars. Hearing this made Billy's head begin to spin. Was it that easy? Could he pull it off? How would he go about selling that much coke?

He had to admit he was in over his head. Maybe his new friend could explain it all to him. He started to ask all the questions but choose not to. He actually felt that this was not the time or place. He was sure that Robert would be more than happy to answer these questions, but he was also sure that that conversation needed to be in a more private setting. With that understood, Billy sat back in his chair and finished his brandy.

As Robert and Billy stepped out of the Excalibur, Jose pulled the Benz up allowing them to step in. Robert asked Billy where he wanted to be dropped off. Billy told him to take him back to the restaurant and then asked if he could come by the Hilton to discuss a few things with Robert. Robert thought about this for a second or two and then said, "No, why don't we just plan on meeting sometime tomorrow evening." Billy said that would be fine as long as they got together because he felt that they really had a lot to talk about. Robert said that would be fine and reminded Billy to do his best to have JD come by The Eatery at a time that he could meet him. Billy acknowledged that he would take care of that and would give him a call to let him know when he was going to be there. After a few minutes, the car came to a stop and the two shook hands and Billy said he would be in touch. After the door shut Robert told Jose to take him back to the Hilton, he was calling it a night.

As Robert stepped inside his suite, the first thing he noticed was the message light was blinking. He smiled before he even called to obtain the message as he figured it was Tina. He was right; she had called about thirty minutes ago and asked him to give her a call if it wasn't too late. Hanging up the phone, he smiled as he dialed her number. When she answered the phone all he needed to do was say hello to get her to start talking. She went on about her night; it seemed that the bar was slow. She had spent six hours and only made about fifty dollars. When she finished complaining about her night, she asked what he had been doing. Robert said he had gone out with Billy for a drink but really had not been doing too much. She asked if he was going to bed, if not she would like to come by. Maybe they could catch a drink or something. This sounded good to Robert and he suggested that she meet him in the bar off the lobby. Tina readily agreed and said she would be there within twenty minutes.

Robert went downstairs and was in the bar when Tina came in. She looked great, wearing an old pair of blue jeans and an off the shoulder shirt, she did look comfortable. She smiled when she saw Robert and came straight over to him. He stood up to greet her and, was met with a kiss. Damn, he was really beginning to like this girl. They sat there in the bar and enjoyed a few drinks and the music that was being played. They talked about first one thing then another, nothing of any real importance, just your normal small talk. It was relaxing to both. They both kept smiling; one would think they were a true couple. After they finished their second Robert asked if Tina would like to go upstairs. The smile that flashed across her face was answer enough.

When they entered Robert's suite neither could keep their hands off the other. They seemed to more like young high school kids rather than two individuals over the age of twenty-one. Finally, Robert broke of the kiss and asked Tina to take a seat on the couch. He went to the wet bar and fixed them both a drink and sat down next to her. Taking her hand in his he asked, "What are you looking for." This question took Tina by surprise, as she really had not given it much thought. She had to admit that to Robert, but went on to say, "I really enjoy being with you and am not opposed to spending as much time together as we could." This brought a smile to Robert's face. He knew he had not thought that much about it either but he also knew he enjoyed being with her. The silence that now engulfed the room was not uncomfortable but it was a bit awkward. The two just sat and smiled. Robert finally broke the silence and asked, "Why are you so upset about only making fifty dollars tonight." Tina put her head down, a little embarrassed, but had to say that she was a little behind on bills and could have used a better night. Robert quickly asked, "How far behind are you?" and had to laugh when he heard she probably was down about a grand. This laughter was not received well on Tina's part and she feigned anger for a bit. The more she complained the more and louder Robert laughed. In a playful manner, Tina began to hit him on the shoulder, which only brought more laughter. Finally, it was too much for Tina to keep this up and she joined him in laughing aloud. The two ended their laughter while embracing in a warm hug.

As they broke the hug with a little kiss, Robert looked into Tina's eyes and said, "Let me take care of your debts." Tina was unsure about this. The last thing she wanted was to be a kept woman. She was proud of the fact that she had always been able to pay her own way and had no problem letting that fact be known. Robert assured her that that was not the case. He just wanted to help her; he was not trying to run her life or anything remotely close to that. If she wanted, she could even consider it a loan. After all, with the events in New York, who knew how long it might be before the L.A. crowd started moving around again. Tina responded to this idea by saying, "Oh yeah, I'm behind about a grand and you want me to go in debt to you for the same amount." Robert said if she would like he could loan her more. This brought a smile to Tina, this really made a lot of sense, borrow more money to be caught up on her bills just to be farther in debt. She had to be honest it was tempting. However, she knew better, borrowing money from the man she was starting to date probably was not a good idea. If this was going to have any chance to grow into a true relationship debt was not a good start. Robert sensed her hesitation and said, "Listen, it was just a thought nothing to loose any sleep over." Nevertheless, deep down inside he was disappointed. He really wanted to help her and did not see how that could be a bad thing. However, if she was not sure, there was no reason to push the idea. The two just sat for a while enjoying their nightcap.

As they were finishing their drinks Robert said that he needed to get to bed. He hoped that Tina would stay but was a bit unsure how to go about making that happen. It had been awhile since he had anyone in is life. Tina smiled and asked, "Would you like me to stay or would you rather be alone?" Robert was relieved by the question. He leaned over and gave her a big kiss. Afterward, he simply asked, "Does that answer your question?" Tina grabbed his hand, stood up and headed toward the bedroom.

Robert was awakened by the sound of his cell phone ringing. Reaching for the phone, he looked at the clock, 11:30am. He hoped it was Billy. Sure enough, Billy was on the other end and was telling him that JD would be in around 1:30. Then he asked if there was anyway that Robert could make it about that time. Robert told him, "I would like to have both of you at a table, he would come in and everything would seem natural. Can you make sure that will happen?" Billy said he could and with that, the conversation was over. After placing the phone back on the nightstand, Robert looked over and saw Tina, laying there with that beautiful smile that he liked so much. She asked if anything was up, to which he said that he had an appointment he had to keep, somewhere between 1:30 and 2:00. The he asked, "What do you have going on today?" Tina responded by saying, "Not much, I don't go in to work until five." Robert laid his head back down and asked if she would like to stay here while he went out. She said that would be fine, but she would need to get by her place before she went to work. And she felt a shower would do her good. Robert said that was fine, he would get her a car around three. Tina agreed to this and Robert headed to the shower.

After Robert was dressed, he called the car service and told them he needed to be leaving by 1:30 and was told that would be fine. He asked if Jose would be driving again and the answer again was what he wanted to hear. He then went out to the living room and found Tina with a pot of coffee. She poured him a cup and asked if it were ok that she had ordered room service. "Of course it was." Robert said. As they sat and enjoyed the coffee, she asked what kind of meeting he was going to. Robert smiled and said that it was just a little business that he had found, nothing too important. It was about time for Robert to head down to the lobby. He bent down and gave Tina a goodbye kiss. Tina said, "Have a good meeting." With that, he was gone.

Robert was glad to see Jose opening the back door to the Benz. As he got to the car, he told him that he would prefer the Benz for the rest of his stay. "The stretch was a bit much, if you know what I mean." Jose said he would take care of it, not to worry. Robert smiled and said he was going to The Eatery. The ride was short, almost too short. Robert really did not have time to plan how he was going to handle the whole thing. Oh well, he thought just improvise.

As he stepped inside, he told the hostess that he needed a table for one, preferably in the smoking section. She smile and said, "Follow me Sir." With that being settled, they began walking towards the back room. Upon entering, he glanced around and saw Billy, and what he thought was JD, sitting at a table in the middle of the room. The hostess stopped at a table in the front and Robert asked if he could have one in the rear. She smiled and said that would be fine. As they headed towards the back of the room, passing the table Billy and JD sat at, Billy looked up and said, "Hello Robert." Robert stopped and shook his hand, following that he introduced Robert to JD and asked if he would like to join them. Robert appeared to be thinking this over and then said if it were all right with JD, he would like that. JD smiled and said that was fine with him. Robert noticed the fact that he really did not like this but agreed anyway. As Robert sat down, he asked how they were doing, just trying to make small talk. Both said they were fine and with that, silence fell upon the table. Robert took a quick look around the room and realized that no one else was there. This made him very comfortable as he figured there was a lot to discuss.

He was not wrong. He had been there for only a few minutes when JD turned to Billy and asked if he was going to be paid today. Billy sat, very stiff and absolutely stoned faced. He did not know what to say, hell, he had no idea what to say. The silence was awkward for each one at the table. Finally JD spoke, "Billy you made the bet, your team lost, you owe." Billy said he was aware of that but he would need more time. This went over like a led balloon. Robert could sense the tension level rise and waited to see how JD reacted. JD sat in silence and then stated, "That is not how I do business, and you need to understand that I need the cash. I am not in the habit of carrying people who owe me money." Billy just sat, staring at JD as if there was no problem. Robert could see where this was going, the bookie was pissed. He came in expecting to be paid, not to be asked for more time. Hell, Robert could understand just how he felt. He had been in similar situations and understood his anger. The silence as they say, was deafening.

As Robert sat and thought about what was playing out in front of him a waiter came to the table and told Billy that he was needed in the kitchen. Without a word spoken, Billy left the table. Now Robert and JD were alone and Robert felt now was the time to go to work. He leaned toward JD and said, "I understand the position you are in, but I feel that you do not totally comprehend what is really going on." To this JD laughed, he did not know this man and he figured he had no clue as to what was going on. He then looked at Robert and said, "You don't know shit about the position I am in, so the best thing you can do is shut the fuck up!" Robert smiled, leaned forward again and said, "You want to get paid for a hundred thousand dollar bet and I am telling you that will not occur for at least a week. As I said, you really do not understand what is going on here."

"Well, if I don't understand then maybe you should explain it to me," responded JD. Robert sat back in his chair, smiled and simply shook his head no. Anyone within twenty feet of these two would have known that the one called JD was at the least confused and at the best pissed, and really pissed. As JD began to speak Robert cut him off and said, "I am the one person who can assure that you get paid, if you give me the time I need to make a few things happen." JD flashed a quick grin and said, "Oh, so you're going to pay off this bums debt?" Robert again shook his head in the negative. JD was unsure how to react to this. He sat and thought but was unable to really gain an understanding of what he was being told. Again, he asked Robert to explain what he meant. Robert again smiled, giving this some time to sink in and finally spoke, "As I said, if you want to get your money I am the man who is going to make that happen. If you do not want your cash that is fine with me, really I do not give a damn about you or your business. However, if you are half the businessman I think you are, you will recognize that you have a problem and I am the only one who can make that problem disappear. In order to do this you need to back off and give me the time that I have already told you was required, again if you do not back off then you do not get paid. I can not make it any more clear than that." JD sat for a moment then smiled and said, "Fine asshole, you want a week, you've got it. But in a week if I do not have my hands on that hundred grand it will be you I come looking for. Now is that clear enough for you?" Robert smiled as if to say he understood and with that, JD got up and made his way to the front door. Robert sat back in his chair, lifted his glass and had a certain smirk on his face. Yes, he was proud of himself, he knew that now Billy would truly be in his debt.

As Robert sat in silence, he wondered if he was on the right track. Hell, he had found his mark, gained his trust, and now was involved with a bookie that was owed one hundred thousand dollars. What was he going to do, he wondered. With these thoughts swimming around in his head, Billy came back to the table. As he was sitting down he asked, "Where is JD?" Robert smiled and looked in a serious manner at Billy and simply said, "He is gone and want be back for a few days." This brought a sigh of relief from Billy. He did not have a clue as to how this new friend had managed to accomplish this, but he was truly grateful. He was not sure how, but, he knew he had to make sure Robert knew what he was feeling. Billy called one of the waiters over and told him to get two steaks both cooked rare, the vegetable medley, mushroom caps and to bring out some Calamari to start things of. Before the young man left, he also told him to bring two Crown and Cokes and to make them doubles. As the waiter left, Billy looked at Robert and smiled. He hoped that Robert understood why he had done what he had done. Robert just smiled.

The late lunch was nice and the conversation had remained simple. The two had talked a little about baseball and football. Everything seemed at ease, but both knew there was an under current that could not be over looked. As Robert finished chewing his last bite, he told Billy that they needed to talk. Billy said he understood and asked exactly what they needed to talk about. Robert leaned forward and said, "Not here, there are too many ears that may be listening." He went on to say he felt his suite would be the best place to discuss what they needed to talk about. Billy agreed that that may be best and offered to come by after he finished here at the restaurant. Robert said that would be fine and for him to call when he was on his way. Billy agreed and the two shook hands and Robert made his way out to the car.

As he approached the Benz, Jose opened the passenger door and asked, "Where to boss?" Robert had to smile at the new name he was being called. His reply was short and to the point, "To the bar he had been at Monday night." Jose smiled saying he understood. Robert, sitting in the back seat wondered if Jose really understood. He had not seen Tina since earlier and he had to admit he was missing her. He was not sure why, he just knew he was. Getting out at The Varsity there was a youthful spring in Roberts' step. As he walked inside he saw Tina talking with some people at a large table, he could see that she was enjoying her work and wondered if maybe he should leave. At that time she saw him and that wonderful smile was now being flashed in his direction. No, he had to think, coming here was the right thing to do.

Robert simply stood and watched Tina work, this brought a smile to his face. It only took her a few moments to make her way to him and she greeted him with a kiss on the cheek. She asked if he wanted a table to which he said only if she were going to take care of him. To this Tina said, "I think I have done a pretty good job of that already, haven't I?" Robert could not help himself from laughing aloud. The smile on his face was enough of an answer for Tina. She grabbed his hand and led him to a table, in the back of course.

Sitting there, watching Tina worked had a relaxing effect on Robert. Damn he thought she was good. After a few minutes, she returned to her favorite guest and asked, "How did your meeting go today." Robert said he had met with a potential client and that the meeting had gone better than he expected. Tina smiled and said. "I would expect nothing less out of you." This brought a smile to Robert. Wow, this girl had gotten under his skin. This was new territory for him, but he liked it. Tina could not help herself; she had to know if they were going to be together later tonight. Robert said he wished that was possible but he had a meeting to get to. He told her he stopped in to see her and that he hoped he could make it up to her. Tina did her best to hide her disappointment but it came through. Robert could see it but choose not to let on. He figured now would be a good time to take the lead so he said, "What do you have planned for tomorrow?" Tina said that she had nothing planned and that she had the next two days off. This caught Robert by surprise as that meant she was not working on the weekend, the two biggest cash days in the life of a waitress. His surprise was easy for Tina to see, and in that, she was pleased. She told him that she had requested the time off in hopes that they could spend some more time together. Robert knew that this might be difficult but said he was sure that they could. Glancing at his watch, he realized that it was close to midnight and knew he needed to get back to the Hilton. He stood up, and gave Tina a hug and a kiss and asked her to give in a call after ten in the morning. Tina said she would, wished him good luck and walked with him to the door. Robert went to give her some money for his drink but Tina told him not to bother, the least she could do was buy him a drink. She gave him another little kiss and told him there would be more when they saw each other again. Robert smiled as he walked outside, getting in the car he told Jose to take him back to the Hilton.

Back in his suite Robert began to think about what would be the best way to get the ball rolling with Billy. Robert decided that a few drinks would come in handy so he called room service and ordered a bottle of Crown, several Cokes, and a bucket of ice with two glasses. He said, "I need them within thirty minutes" and was told that would not be a problem. Not too long after he had hung up the phone there was a knock on the door. As he looked through the peephole, he saw Billy standing there. Opening the door, he invited Billy in. The two shook hands and took seats in the living room area. The conversation was really about nothing, small talk for the most part. Then Billy asked about Tina, he wanted to know how Robert was able to accomplish something that no other man, at least that Billy had seen, had been able to do. To this, Robert just smiled, as if to say that this was not something to be discussed. Billy understood, but was a little disappointed. At this time, there came another knock on the door and Billy jumped in uncomfortable surprise. Robert told him not to worry it was just room service. After closing the door, Robert asked Billy if he would like a drink. Billy said that would be nice. Now the two sat with drinks in hand, Billy asked, "Please explain to me how this whole thing that you brought up at The Eatery worked" Robert sat back and appeared to be in deep thought. The silence was not a comfort to Billy. He really wanted an answer to his question. Looking at Robert, he realized that he could not force the issue. This man, his new friend, held all the cards. No matter how much he wanted to be in control he had to admit that he was not. This fact did nothing to ease how he felt, but it was the way things were. Finally, Robert began to speak. "It really is not all that difficult. If you really want to make the deal, the first thing that must happen is the cash needs to be made available. Secondly, I will contact the people I know to set up the buy. Now one thing must be understood and agreed to, that was there was no way that I will allow the cash and the drugs to ever be in the same place." Billy did not understand this, why would the cash and drugs need to be kept separate. How does one go about buying this amount of cocaine and the cash not there? Billy offered these questions to Robert and truly hoped he would get an answer. Robert had heard these questions many times in the past. He was prepared to hear them but played it slow. He did not want Billy to notice the fact that he was ready for the questions just offered by him. After a few moments had passed Robert began to speak. "First, what you need to understand is that to make sure no one could figure out what was going on that the two needed to be kept separate. This way, friends, employees, and most importantly, cops, would not put two and two together. Secondly, I have set up several of these deals, no one has ever been busted, and I expect to continue that record. Lastly, if you do not feel comfortable with how I do things you can put a stop to it right now and it will be nothing more than talk. Besides, I am not the one with the problem." Billy allowed the words to be digested by his mind. The more he thought about what he had been told the more sense it made. He stood up and began to pace around the room. This was nothing Robert had not seen before. He often wondered why people felt the need to pace, did it really help them think or was it just a way to burn off excess energy. Hell, what did it matter he thought. The answer was it really did not matter as long as they agreed. No sooner than that thought had left his mind did Billy turn and begin to speak. "Ok, I think I understand. My next question is how do I move the coke?" Robert seemed puzzled by this. "Are you trying to get me to believe that you know no one who sells drugs in this town?" Billy had to smile, he too found it hard to believe, but in truth, he did not. Telling this to Robert brought a loud laugh from him. Billy had to laugh also.

"What the hell am I going to do? He asked. Robert gave this some thought and replied, "I am not sure, maybe the people I know can be of some help with this also. Of course this may cost a bit more." Billy said that might work, besides if they already have some people doing the dirty work it would make it that much more easy for him. Of course, he wondered if they could be trusted with the money. To this Robert said, "This is what these people do, they needed to be trusted or else they did not work and earn a living." This brought laughter from Billy. He found it odd that Robert viewed what these people do was a normal job. Hell, they spent their lives outside or rather on the wrong side of the law. With these thoughts, he began to wonder if they had medical and dental along with their jobs. The more he thought about it the more he laughed. Robert asked what was so funny and Billy simply said it was nothing just some stupid thoughts. Robert knew better, but was not going to push the subject.

Having explained the how that this worked, Robert was ready to get things going. He turned to Billy, who had finally sat back down, and asked, "How much do you think you can come up with?" Billy did not hesitate, "Half a million would be about all I can swing." Robert then asked how long it would take him to get the cash to him. Billy said it would take a few days, he needed to cash a few things in and that would take some time. Robert reminded Billy that time was a luxury that he really did not have. "Thanks for reminding me of something that I did not already know, asshole." Robert could only smile at this; damn it seemed that Billy might just have a backbone after all. Robert also had to smile at being called an asshole, how many times had that been thrown in his direction. Hell if he got paid for that one he probably would not have to do what he did.

With all of this out in the open there was little more to do at this time. Robert told Billy as much and said that all he needed to do was start the process of getting the cash. He would make the phone calls that he needed to so that he could get everything in the works. He told Billy that he needed to understand that once that bell had been rung that it was extremely difficult to be undone. He then inquired too make sure Billy understood that. Billy nodded his head indicating that he did. Robert said he hoped so because these people were worse than the IRS or some small time bookie called JD. This really got Billy's attention. That fact was easy for Robert to see. The look in Billy's eyes was exactly the looked he hoped to see. Fear is a great emotion. Nothing else Robert had found before caused so much action. Billy said he understood and told Robert not to make the call until he got his hands on the cash. Robert agreed, saying that was what he intended to do; besides he knew not to set something like this up before he knew he could go through with it. Besides, he did not want to piss of the people that he dealt with. With all of this, being said and apparently understood Robert said it would be a good time for Billy to leave. He told Billy to make sure and not tell anyone about this, as no one else needed to know. That would be the best way to cause everything to fall apart or worse get someone busted. Billy said he understood and he had told no one about any of this. Robert smiled, shook Billy's hand, and opened the door for Billy to leave.

Robert sat down on the couch with a fresh drink in hand. Turning the television set on all he could find was news. Hell, even *ESPN* was not broadcasting. How much longer were the attacks going to consume the American psyche? He had to admit that this was a terrible thing, but give a man a break; any break would be welcomed relief. He turned the set off and reached for the radio, scanning the dial he found a station that was playing music he liked. This was nice. It was better than the news, which simply continued repeating the same thing over and over again. With the music playing his thoughts soon turned to Tina.

Why this girl was taking so much of his thoughts, he wondered. He had to honest with himself he liked her. How much he was unsure, but the fact that he did could not be disputed. It had been a long time since he had felt anything for anyone. This made him uncomfortable and happy at the same time. As he thought about all of this, a smile was on his face. Had he fallen for her, he wondered. He had no answer to that, all he knew was he liked her and liked spending time with her. He decided that he was not going to be able to figure this one out. No, he would just have to let things play out and see where they took him. With that being understood, he got up and made his way to the bedroom. As he laid his head down upon the pillows, his last thought was she would be calling in a few hours. The smile on his face did not diminish as he fell asleep.

As the phone rang Robert looked at the clock beside the bed, 9:00am, he answered the wake up call hoping that Tina would call at ten as they had discussed. He got out of bed and headed towards the shower. Getting out of the shower, he heard his cell phone ringing. He raced for the phone, answering it, he expected to hear Tina's voice, but it was Billy. He asked if he woke Robert up, and when he heard that he had not he wanted to know if they could get together sometime today. This was exactly what Robert did not want to hear. He had hoped that he could spend the entire day with Tina. He asked Billy what was going on and why did they need to get together today. Billy told him that JD had just called and was really laying it on heavy. Robert thought about this for a moment and said, "Give me his number; I'll give him a call. I'll call you back after I have talked to him and in the meantime, relax." Billy was relieved to hear this and he gladly gave Robert the number. After saying goodbyes, Robert finished getting dressed and went to the living room area to make the call.

JD answered on the second ring. Robert said, "I want to know what the hell is going on and why you had called Billy this morning." JD said, "He did not have to explain himself to anyone especially to you." Robert reminded him of their last conversation and said he thought they had an understanding. JD said he remembered their last talk but did not feel they had anything like an understanding. JD then said, "Billy owes me a ton of money and I need to get what is mine." Robert reminded JD that there was no way Billy could pay him now and that he needed to wait at least a week. He tried to assure JD that he would get his money all he needed to do was be patient and allow him to help Billy get his hands on the cash. After more back and forth JD reluctantly agreed but told Robert he was going to hold Robert responsible for the debt if Billy did not make it good. Robert said that was fine. Anything to get this idiot out of the way, anyway all he wanted to do was get ready to be with Tina. After hanging up with JD he called Billy and told him everything was ok and not to worry. JD had agreed to wait for a week and besides he had told JD that if the problem continued he would make it good. Billy could not believe his ears. Did this person, who he had known for only five days, volunteer to get on the hook for his debt. All he could do was thank Robert over and over again until Robert told him to stop. Robert told Billy that he would catch up with him later in the weekend but for the time being he would not be around so don't call. Billy said, "That would be fine but please give him a call as soon as could. Robert said he would and hung up the phone.

It was now five till ten so he rushed to get dressed. No sooner than he had gotten his shoes on when the room phone rang. Answering, he heard Tina saying, "Good morning." Robert responded in kind and asked if she was ready for a good time. Tina gave a little chuckle and said that she was more than ready. Then she asked if he was dressed, Robert said he was and Tina then said, "Well then why don't you just open the damn door and let me in." This caught Robert by surprise but he hung up the phone and went to the door. As he opened it up Tina came walking in. In her hands were two cups of coffee and a bag of pastries. All Robert could do was stand there and shake his head. It seemed that she had thought of everything.

    They gave each other a kiss and sat down together on the couch. After taking a big gulp of coffee Robert asked Tina if she had planned the rest of the day or just breakfast. Tina laughed and said, "No silly, the rest of the day is up to you, but she thought he might enjoy a little something to get the day started." Robert smiled, which brought a smile to Tina's face. She was pleased that her efforts were appreciated. After they finished their coffees and pastries, Robert asked Tina if there was anything she wanted to do. Tina said, "I have been thinking about that last night and most of this morning and to be honest I have not come up with a single idea." Robert smiled and told her that was not a problem, he had an idea. He reached for the phone and called the car service. He was told that Jose would be there with half an hour. He turned to Tina and asked if she would mind taking a little road trip. "I'm up for that, but where do you have in mind?" Tina asked. Robert just said, "Relax and go with the flow."

Soon they found themselves heading down to the lobby, as they walked they were holding hands and talking without saying much. They saw Jose standing next to the Benz as they stepped outside. Robert waited outside as Tina got in, and then he turned to Jose and said, "Feel like making the drive to Vegas?" Jose said they would be there in about three and a half hours. Robert said that would be fine. Getting in, Tina wanted to know what was planned. Robert just smiled and reminded what he had said earlier, "Relax and go with the flow!" Tina could only smile. As she sat there, holding Robert's hand, she could only wonder where they were going. She thought back to the first night they had met and almost could not contain her laughter as she remembered thinking this guy was a loser because he had to call someone for a ride. Boy had she almost blown it, big time.

It did not take Jose long to get out of the city. As they drove through the mountains and entered the desert, Tina had tried to guess where they were going. Robert would just smile at each of her guesses; he had already determined that even if she guessed right he was not going to tell her. Why ruin the surprise. He felt confident that she had not been to Vegas, at least that is what he hoped. He did enjoy allowing a person to do something new. For some reason he was just a little bit more excited about doing it with Tina. He really did like being with her. They had been driving for about two and a half to three hours and Robert leaned over the front seat and whispered in Jose ear, "The Mirage." Jose smiled and nodded letting Robert know that he understood.

A few miles outside of Vegas Tina spotted a sign advertising one of the hotel casino deals in the city. Excitedly she turned to Robert and said, "Vegas, oh boy I can't wait. I have always wanted to go to Vegas, but never seemed to have the time or the money." Robert smiled and said, "Well I guess you hit the jackpot. I figured we could do a little gambling, get something to eat, catch a show, get some sleep and do it all over again. How does that sound?" he asked. All Tina could do was smile. She had so longed to make the trip to Vegas and now she was getting to do it with someone she truly wanted to be with. He was right she had hit the jackpot.

As they pulled into the Mirage and parked at the front door a valet opened the door and greeted the two of them. He asked if they were here for the day or if they would be staying the night. Robert said they would be here for the night and the young man asked them to follow him to the front desk. Robert signaled for Jose to come with them. Once inside he told Jose that he would get him a room, handed him two one hundred dollar bills and wished him good luck. Jose was shocked, first this man bought him dinner and now a Saturday night in Vegas, damn he thought he too had hit the jackpot. After getting his room key Jose said he needed to call the service to let them know what was going on. Robert said if there was any problem to let him know so he could take care of it. Jose smiled and said, "I doubt that there will be any problem boss." Again, Robert had to smile about the title that Jose insisted on calling him. They shook hands and went their separate ways. Tina and Robert went up to their room. Tina was just a little surprised when she saw the suite that Robert had gotten. The view was unbelievable, so much so that she felt she could stand there for hours just taking it all in.

Robert walked up behind her and reached over her shoulder to hand her a drink. She turned and gave him a nice kiss. This brought a huge smile to Robert's face, he was happy that she was pleased. Just as he went to say as much there was a knock on the door. Tina gave a puzzled looked to Robert and all he did was shrug his shoulders. He went to the door and as he opened it, a distinguished looking gentleman entered. He reached for Robert's hand and shook it as if he was a long time friend. Smiling, he said he was glad to see Robert again and then asked how long it had been. Robert smiled and said, "Too long my old friend. It surely is great seeing you. How are the Misses and the kids?" The man smiled and said the family is doing great and thanked him for asking. Looking at Tina the gentleman smiled, looked at Robert who nodded, and he walked over and introduced himself. "I am Alberto, the hotel manager and I wish to welcome you to my fine hotel." Tina smiled, extended her hand and gave him her name. She thanked him for the hospitality and said she liked what she had seen so far. Jorge smiled then turned to Robert and asked, "Would you like your normal line of credit?" Robert smiled and said that would be fine. Alberto assured him that everything would be taken care of and for him not to worry about a thing. Robert asked if his friend could set him up with tickets for a show. To which Albert replied, "I will get your normal table set up for you, for the eleven o'clock show. David Copperfield is in town and he hoped that they would enjoy the show." Robert said he was sure they would and again thanked him. Alberto then asked what he had been up to and was told that Robert was spending some time in L.A. and had just wanted to get out of the city for a couple of days. Alberto noticed that they had no luggage and offered to have someone from the clothing store to come up with a selection for them to choose. Robert looked at Tina, she was just standing there smiling and he said that would be fine. Alberto headed for the door and told them to stay in the room and he would have one of the ladies bring some clothes up. Again, Robert thanked him, they shook hands and he was gone,

Tina could not believe what had transpired in the past few hours. It seemed like just a few hours ago they were drinking coffee in Robert's suite in L.A. and now here they were in Vegas and Robert was being treated like a king. She smiled at that thought, as she realized that if he was a king then she must be a queen. Robert could sense that she was a little overwhelmed and walked over to her and gave her a long hug. As the two embraced, Tina did feel like a queen, she was having a little trouble grasping everything that had changed in her life since this man walked into the Varsity just last Monday night.

She had allowed herself to relax around a man, something she had not done in sometime. Not only had she relaxed she had actually given herself to him. This had been nice. She realized just how much she liked spending time with him. She was not sure to what extent but she did know that she liked him. She remembered what he had told her that morning, "Relax and go with the flow." She had to admit, that was damn good advice. Go with the flow that was exactly what she was going to do. No sense in trying to understand everything, it was just a little overwhelming, but damn she did like it. Liked it all. Robert looked at Tina and asked if everything was all right. All she could do was smile.

As the two stood in the middle of the living area of the suite enjoying the embrace there came a knock on the door. Robert broke the embrace, and went to open the door. In walked a woman with what appeared to be a luggage rack full of clothes. There were casual clothes, suits, shoes, and even underwear. Tina could not believe what she was seeing. This entire trip was somewhat surreal. As she stepped over to look at the clothes, she could not believe that all the ladies clothes were her size. Alberto must really know what he was doing. Robert had taken a tuxedo, he said for the show, a couple of pairs of slacks, and three or four casual shirts. He told Tina to take whatever she wanted and with that handed her a long dress, smiled and said for the show. Tina had never been in any situation that even remotely resembled this. She was not sure how to act, hell she was not even sure if her reactions were the right ones. All she knew was, she liked the way she was being treated and deep down inside hoped it would never end.

After changing, they headed downstairs for the casino. Tina was holding Robert's hand and she asked what games he liked to play. Robert smiled and said, "Blackjack, besides it was the only game that the odds were not completely stacked in favor of the house. Have you ever played?" he asked. Tina said, "I have given it a try once but I sucked." She told him that she had started with two hundred dollars and had lost it all in about a half hour. Robert laughed and told her it was a good start, with that he told her that she needed to sit next to him, watch, ask questions, and learn. She said that would be fine with her.

As they sat down at a table, a man in a suit came over and handed Robert a tray full of chips. He thanked the man for the chips and handed a stack to Tina. She looked down and saw that each on had $1000 stamped on it. She could not believe her eyes. She looked at Robert and said, "I just told you how badly I suck at this game and you want me to play with chips worth a thousand dollars, have you taken total leave of your senses or what." Robert did not even try to hold back the laughter. He smiled and told her to just play and have fun. It really did not matter if she won or lost as long as she had fun. Tina shrugged her shoulders, what the hell she thought it was not her money. That thought did not make her feel good. She cared for Robert, and did not want to take advantage of him. She did not think she was, but she also did not want him to think that she was. She told Robert, "I am not comfortable gambling with your money." Robert smiled, grabbed her hand, gave her a kiss and said, "Sweetie its just money don't worry about a thing. I am giving it too you, no strings attached. You can gamble it, cash it in, do whatever you want to. It is yours now, and by the way, if you win that belongs to you also." Tina was completely blown away. No one just hands out fifty thousand dollars and wants nothing in return. Nevertheless, Robert was different she already knew that. Then she remembered what he had told her earlier, "Relax and go with the flow." She smiled and said, "I will just go with the flow." Robert smiled and wished her good luck.

Tina did not play the first two or three hands, instead she watched Robert. She was trying to learn how he played the game. What she learned was this man had to be the luckiest player in the place. Each bet was ten thousand dollars, and he won all three hands. The first two were Blackjacks and the third; he doubled down on an ace/six and hit the five. Unreal, was all she could think. Finally, she gathered the courage to place one chip in the betting circle. Her cards came and they were each an ace. Robert had seventeen showing the dealer had a two. Robert looked at her and told her to split the aces and put one more chip out there with the second ace. Doing as she was told the dealer placed one card on the first ace it was a ten. Then he did the same to the second one, again a ten. The dealer then turned over his second card, a ten. He announced that he had to take a hit, the card was a three, fifteen. The dealer then said he was taking his next card, a king, "Dealer bust, every player wins." Tina screamed out loud, she was so excited. She could not believe her luck. Wow, in less than two minutes she had won several grand, unbelievable. Robert gave her a little kiss and told her to keep it up. They continued to play for several hours and finally Robert asked if she was ready to get a bite to eat. Tina smiled, and said she thought he would never ask. Robert asked for someone to take care of their chips and a man came with some trays and collected all of their chips. He told Robert that he would have a receipt for them whenever he was ready. Robert said that would be fine and the two of them headed out of the casino.

Tina asked where they were going to dinner, in the hotel or somewhere else. Robert said he knew of a real nice steakhouse within walking distance and asked if that would be fine or did Tina care for something else. She said that would be fine. They walked down the strip a couple of blocks then took a side street for a few blocks. They passed by several small casinos and a few low rate motels. Just about the time Tina was beginning to feel uncomfortable, she saw what she thought was a restaurant in the next block. As they got closer, she discovered she was correct. Robert pulled her close to him as they reached the door. Pushing it open, they stepped inside something that seemed straight out of the old west. A gentleman came up to them and asked how many, Robert replied it would be just the two of them and if possible they would prefer a table in the smoking section. The man smiled and asked them to follow him. As they walked through the restaurant, the aroma of the food made both of their mouths water. Tina looked at each table and it seemed that every plate was covered with the largest piece of meat she had ever seen. She figured that there was no way she could ever eat that much food. As they got to their table, they sat down and Robert pointed to a chalkboard on a nearby wall. That was the menu. It showed three steaks, a porterhouse weighing 36 ounces, a ribeye weighing 24 ounces, and a fillet weighing 18 ounces. Each came with a baked potato, pinto beans, corn on the cob, and a salad. Tina turned and looked at Robert and asked, "Are you kidding or just trying to fatten me up for the kill?" Robert laughed and said, "The food was excellent and if she would rather they could split one." This sounded great to Tina as she now knew there was no way she could eat one of these steaks. With that being decided, they would split a ribeye and the sides. They ordered a couple of Crown and Cokes along with their dinner. Tina looked at Robert and asked how he had done at the table. Robert smiled and said he thought he was up a little bit. The two sat and talked about everything they had seen while being in Vegas. Tina really felt like a tourist. She was full of questions and was pleased that Robert had answers for each question she asked. The more they talked the more she understood just how close they were becoming. She thought that for knowing this man for less than a week she really felt close to him. She hoped that he felt the same way. She wanted to know but was afraid to ask, she wanted to, but the fear that she may be miss reading everything was too great to over come. With that thought she decided to let it go for now, remembering what he had said earlier, "Relax and go with the flow." Those words made so much sense.

As the two sat and ate, the conversation became a little more serious. Robert had asked just what Tina was looking for, was this just a fun spree or was there the possibility of something deeper. Tina tried her best to do a soft-shoe around the question but Robert would not allow her that luxury. Even though she did her best not to commit, he continued to push for an answer. When she tried to ask him the same question he replied, "It is not nice to answer a question with a question." Tina had always hated that response, she took a deep breath, looked into his eyes, and said, "All I know is I like you very much and to be totally honest with you I hope that something deeper might come of all of this." Robert smiled and told her he felt the same way. Hearing this made Tina feel very nice, it was almost like feeling warm water wash over her. All she could do was smile.

At that time, their dinner arrived and no one was more grateful than Tina was. She really was not good in dealing with talking about true feelings, but she had to admit it was easy with Robert. She did not quite understand this but what the hell; relax and go with the flow, right. As they were finishing their meal Robert glanced at his watch and told her, they needed to head back to the Mirage, as the show would be starting soon. With that being said, they took care of the bill and began making their way back to the Mirage. They had only been walking for about one full block when suddenly a man jumped out of a shadow with a knife in his hand. Tina tried to scream but nothing came out of her mouth. The man demanded their money and jewelry and upon saying this, he swung the knife in a threatening manner. Robert pulled Tina behind him so that he was standing between her and the knife. Tina was petrified and really could not grasp what was happening to them. Then Robert did something that caught her totally by surprise, he reached into the left side of his blazer and pulled out a pistol. He looked at the man and said, "Just like a redneck, bring a knife to a gun fight." The mans eyes became the size of silver dollars and he turned and ran away as fast as he could. Robert returned the pistol to where it had come from and turned to make sure Tina was all right. She was visibly shaken but otherwise she seemed ok. After she had calmed down she looked at Robert and asked where the gun came from. Robert told her he usually carried his 9mm just to be on the safe side. She had to agree that this time it probably was a good thing. Tina said that they should call the police but Robert said it was not necessary. No one had been hurt, the man had only put a scare into them and he got one in return. Besides Robert said, "I doubt that fool would be pulling his knife on anyone for sometime." As he said this both he and Tina had to laugh, it was probably a very true statement. She still thought contacting the police would be smart but Robert would have nothing to do with it. She decided to let it go, as he was so passionate about not bothering the police. With this being settled they began heading for the Mirage but this time Tina make sure she held on to Roberts arm. There was no way she was going to let her hero get away.

As the entered the Mirage, Tina felt the definite feeling of relief. There was not a better feeling than to be with Robert and be back in the safety of the major hotel. They found themselves entering the grand ballroom for the David Copperfield show and were escorted to their table. Tina was not surprised that they were sitting front row, dead center of the stage. They had only been seated for a few minutes when a waitress came by with a bottle of champagne, Moet Chadon Whitestar. They were told that the bottle was from Alberto. Robert smiled and asked her to make sure that Alberto was told thank you. Again, Tina was not surprised. She was starting to understand that Robert knew many people and it seemed that most liked and respected him. She could understand that, as she felt the same but, she found it unusual that so many people not only knew this man but also appeared to have some sort of relationship with him. There was no need to spend much time thinking about this Tina decided. The waitress had opened the bottle and poured each a glass. Robert raised his and he asked, "What should we toast to." Tina smiled and said she had a good one. With that she raised her glass and said, "Relax and go with the flow." This brought a smile to Robert's face, they brought their glasses together softly, and with each of them smiling, they took their first sip. Tina was surprised, this champagne was very nice, she could get real used to this she thought.

Before they had finished their fast glass, the lights dimmed and the show began. Being this close to a world-class magician was unbelievable.

One would think that being this close you could see how the tricks were done. Tina realized very quickly that this man was more unbelievable in real life than on television. As the show went on, she allowed herself to become lost in the entertainment. It was nice to sit for ninety minutes and not to have to think about anything except what she was seeing or rather not seeing. As the lights were brought back up, she really was not ready for the show to end. But alas, end it had and Robert reached for her hand, after doing so he asked what she thought. All she could say was how amazed she was. She went on to explain just how unreal the whole show was, she had to admit she had been completely fooled by each of his tricks. Robert had to agree he had not been able to see anything that would have given away any of the tricks.

As they stood to leave, Robert gave her a slight hug and kissed. Tina felt special, yes, she was right when she had told him earlier that she hoped something deeper would develop between the two of them.

It did not take long for them to reach their suite. Once inside they found two chip trays, one contained what appeared to be about seventy thousand dollars and the other about ten thousand. Robert picked up the smaller one and handed it to Tina. Tina looked confused and Robert said this is your winnings. Tina looked at him as if to say you're kidding. Robert smiled and said, "Don't you remember, I told you what you won was yours." Tina said there was no way she could keep this money. Robert playfully acted upset and hurt by what she had said. It took Tina a few minutes to realize that he was playing with her. All she could do was laugh at him; she had to admit she did find him funny. After talking about this situation, Tina finally agreed to accept the money. Robert had done an excellent job of making sure she understood that she had won that money fair and square and he had lost nothing by providing her with the money to play with. With this being settled the two lovers made their way to the bedroom.

Robert was the first to awake and he left the bed as quietly as he could. He went into the living area and called room serviced. He ordered a pot of coffee, danishes, bagels, scrambled eggs, bacon, sausage, and plain toast. He was told that the food would arrive within thirty minutes and he said that would be fine. He then called down to the front desk and asked to be connected to Jose's room. The phone rang a few times before Jose answered. Robert asked if he was sleeping and was told no he had just been in the bathroom. Robert asked how his evening had been. Jose said everything had gone very well and again thanked Robert for being so kind. Robert said not to worry about it and he did not need to thank him anymore. He had done what he did because he wanted to and that was all there was to it. Robert then told Jose that they should plan to leave for L.A. around eleven and wanted to make sure this would give Jose enough time. Jose looked at the clock and seeing it was only 8:30am he assured Robert that would not be a problem. Robert thanked him and said they would be in the lobby at eleven.

Hanging up the phone, he could hear Tina moving around in the bedroom. As she came out, he met her at the door and gave her a big kiss and hug. Tina smiled and told him she could get use to that every morning. This brought a huge smile to Roberts face, hearing this from her really made him happy. Looking into her eyes he said, "Well, we just might have to see what we need to do to make that happen on a more frequent manner." Hearing this made Tina smile; it also gave rise to thoughts of what was meant by more frequent, was he thinking about living together or what. Did she dare ask, again she did not know. All she could do was stand there and smile.

Soon there was a knock on the door and Robert said breakfast has arrived. He opened the door and a waiter rolled a large cart into the room. Tina could see several covered dishes on the cart along with a large carafe of what she assumed was coffee. Robert asked the man to set the cart up between the two chairs and that would be fine. With this being done the waiter left and Robert invited Tina over for breakfast. As she sat down Robert began to remove the covers on the food. While he was doing this Tina poured two cups of coffee and then just watched. She was amazed at all the food and she said so. Robert smiled and said he was not sure what she liked for breakfast so he did the best thing he could, order one of everything. All Tina could do was smile. This man was unreal, god she hoped the other shoe never dropped, this was too real and too good, and she did not want it to end. She was beginning to think she was falling in love. This was definitely something she had never felt before. Oh sure she had suffered through that puppy love thing back at the age of sixteen but nothing since that time. All she knew was she did not want any of this to end it was too real, too good, too right. Again, all she could do was smile.

The trip back to L.A. went with out a hitch. The talk between Robert and Tina centered on the happenings in Vegas. Both were very relaxed and neither wanted to push the subject about where the relationship was headed. As they were just getting to the city, Robert turned to Tina and asked, "Where do wish to be dropped off, your place or would you rather come back to the Hilton with me?" Tina's surprise was very evident, especially to some one like Robert who had made his fortune from reading people. After she had collected herself, she smiled and offered, "I know what I would like to do but what would you prefer?" Robert could not stop from smiling, "If it were up to me I would just as soon have you with me full time, I am just unsure what you what." Tina took a deep breath and said, "Well if it is truly up to me I guess I would like to go by my place and pick up a few things. Certainly would not want to make you have to support a lowly little waitress." This brought a chuckle from Robert. He quickly said, "First of all, you are anything but a lowly little waitress, secondly, you did just win a little over ten thousand dollars, and lastly, I just want you with me, I do not care if I need to spring for a complete new wardrobe or not." Tina response was nothing more than a big hug and passionate kiss. In less than forty-five minutes the two where in Roberts' suite at the Hilton. If anyone had been paying attention in the hotel lobby, they would have thought two newlyweds had just walked by. The affection was true and overflowing. Back in the suite, Robert and Tina were in the living area when Robert's cell phone rang.

Robert looked at the caller id and recognized the number it was The Eatery. He answered and call and Billy said, "Are you back in town?" This took Robert by surprise, "What do you mean am I back in town, Billy?"

"I came by your suite both last night and this morning. I usually figure if someone is not in during a ten hour period then they are having one hell of a good time or they have left town for some reason." Robert really did not like what he was hearing. He was not used to having a mark keep track of him, at least not this early in the scam. Not wanting to let on that he was upset he laughed and told Billy that he had made a quick run to Las Vegas, no big deal. Then he asked, "What can I do for you, my friend?" Billy was caught off guard; being called friend was something that he had longed for, especially from Robert. With a smile in his voice he stated, "I was hoping you had a few minutes to discuss the things that we were talking about towards the end of last week."

"I really don't think there is anything more to talk about. The only thing that needs to happen is you need to come up with your end and then everything will begin to fall into place. You just need to stay calm and let things happen the way they need to happen. Do you understand?" Billy listened to everything that Robert had said, he did not like it but he had to agree. He told Robert that he would be in touch sometime this week and asked him to keep in touch. Robert said he would and reminded Billy that he just needed to relax everything would be all right.

After he hung up the phone, he looked at Tina who had been listening intently to the conversation. Before Robert could say anything Tina stood up, and looking in his direction, she asked, "Was that Billy from The Eatery?" Robert just looked at her and smiled. Tina was quick to pick on the fact that she was entering an area of uncharted waters. She thought long and hard about pushing the subject and decided that she would be better off letting these sleeping dogs alone. Smiling back at Robert, Tina said, "Listen, obviously it is none of my business. I can live with that." Robert, still smiling stepped over to her, gave her a hug and said, "There is a lot that we don't know about each other. Most of these things will come out in time, please just be patient, alright?" Tina returned the hug and said she understood and agreed that in time they would probably know just about everything about one another. Robert moved towards the bar, fixing each a cocktail, he breathed a sigh of relief. He really was not comfortable talking about what he had going on, and he really had no intentions to involve her in his business. Besides, this was going to be his last score; after it was finished, the two of them would be able to get their lives together. If at that point in time, there was ever a need to discuss what he used to do, so be it.

Handing Tina her drank he sat down beside her and asked, "Ok, you choose to come back here with me, what is the next move?" Tina took a slow drink, sat her glass down on a nearby table, looked at Robert, and said, "I really have not given that much thought. Let me ask you this, are looking for someone to be with while you are here in L.A. or are you looking for something more?" Robert took a deep breath and said, "Wow, you know how to get to the point, don't you? Well I guess I owe you an answer. I am not sure what I am looking for; all I know for sure is I like being with you and I know anytime we are apart I wish you were with me. I have enjoyed the time we have spent together and I do not want it to end. How is that for an answer?" Tina smiled and said, "Robert, I like you also, I too have enjoyed the time that we have spent together, and I too do not want it to end. All I am saying is I am not sure exactly what it is between us. Do you want me to move out of my condo, because if you do then I need to know that this is not just fun for a month. Do you want

THE FINAL SCORE

me to stop working at The Varsity and if so how am I supposed to support myself? Wow, you're right, I do know how to get to the point." With that being said, both sat back and laughed. The laughter was not the nervous type; no, it was more that each had understood wear they had gotten. This was real, just how real was the question.

After they finished their drinks, they decided to order pizza for dinner. As they sat and ate, all Tina could think about was what they had discussed or actually had not discussed earlier. She really wanted to bring it all up again but was concerned that Robert would get upset. She decided to just let it go, for now. Robert was having the same thoughts. He really wanted to answer Tina's questions; he just did not know how to go about it. Understanding this brought nothing but anger to him. He was the person who could talk to anybody about anything. He was the one who knew all the answers, knew just what to say and when to say it. Damn he was confused. Must be the girl, he thought. Then he decided what the hell, turning to Tina he smiled and began talking. "Tina, listen about what you asked earlier, how do you want to handle all of this?" Tina laughed, "Why is it that I am them one that has to answer these questions, why don't you tell me how you want to handle things." Robert laughed, "Damn we make one hell of a couple don't we. I mean we both have something to talk about and neither one of us seems to really want to get into it. OK, here goes nothing, Yes, I want you to get the hell out of that condo, yes, I want you to tell the Varsity to find someone else to push the last legal drug, and most importantly, I want you living with me until you decide you can't put up with me anymore. So how about them apples?" Needles to say, Tina was blown away, all she could do was sit and smile. Finally, she looked at Robert and said, "I like those apples a lot, how about that?"

"Well I guess we need to get your shit out of the condo, and stop by The Varsity and give them the good news." Again Tina laughed. She could not believe what she was hearing, was this really happening. She gave Robert the biggest hug and kiss she could muster. For the first time since she left Canada she was happy, damn, it felt good. With all the cards, seemingly on the table, they headed to the bedroom.

After Tina and Robert got up and had breakfast, they called the car service and asked for Jose to drive them. Within thirty minutes, they found themselves at the condo that Tina had been in for the past six months. Tina went in to discuss leaving with the manager while Robert went up to her unit to begin the process of moving her out. In no time at all Tina was in her place and she explained to Robert that the manager said she still owed this months rent and would forfeit her deposit for leaving with out giving a thirty day notice. Robert asked how much rent was and when Tina said eight hundred he pulled his money clip out of his pocket and handed her the cash and told her to go take care of it. When she returned, she told Robert that all she wanted to take was some of her clothes and rest she would donate to the next tenant. With that Tina grabbed a couple of suitcases, threw some clothes in each and they left.

The next stop was The Varsity. Tina went inside to tell everyone she was quitting. Robert stayed in the car saying it would go better if he was not with her. Alone, he took advantage of the privacy and made a few phone calls. First, he called Billy. Once he got him on the line he asked, "When do you think you will have your end taken care of?"

"I think I will be able to have it all together by Friday. If that is the case, when will everything be in place?" Robert told him he could not begin to set things in motion until he had the cash in place. Billy said he understood and would be in touch as soon as he was ready. Ending that call, Robert then dialed the number of his banker in Aruba. He hated making international calls; they always seemed to take so much time being connected. Finally, his banker picked up. Robert told him he as in L.A. and he needed some money wired to him. What he was told was the last thing he expected to hear. "I am sorry Mr. Robert, but with all the problems in New York there was no way a wire transfer could go through." Robert reminded him that he was in L.A. and said just send it out here. The banker tried to explain that all wires go through New York and until everything was restored, there was nothing he could do. To which Robert said he understood but also stated he really needed some money. The banker asked him where he was staying and when he heard the Hilton, he asked for a room number. Robert gave him his suite number and was told to expect a package from FedEx; it should be there within forty-eight hours. The banker told him to make sure to let the front desk know that he was expecting a package and ask that they sign for it. Robert smiled, as he understood. By having the front desk sign for it, it removed him from the equation if anyone ever wanted to do some checking. He told his banker, "Send at least one hundred thousand, no better make that two hundred thousand, I don't want to get caught low again." The banker said he would take care of everything. No sooner had he hung up his cell did Tina step into the car.

As Jose got in behind the wheel, he asked where they wanted to go. Tina said she would like to go back to the hotel so she could put her clothes away and Robert agreed.

As they entered the lobby, Robert gave his key card to Tina and said, "I needed to talk to the front desk, go ahead up, I be up in a few minutes." Tina took the key card, gave him a kiss and said, "Don't be too long." The way she said it and with that cute little smile Robert knew she was up to something. He could just figure what she was thinking. He had to admit, he liked the idea. Stepping up to the front desk Robert told the young person there that he expected a package from FedEx and hoped that someone there could sign for it. She told Robert that that would not be a problem as they do this type of thing for guest all the time. Robert smiled; she then asked if there was anything else she could do for him. Robert said yes, he needed another key for his suite. Again, the young woman was more than happy to take care of his needs. Robert thanked her and headed for the elevator. As he pushed the button to call the elevator, he felt something sharp at his left side.

Hearing the voice of JD was the last thing Robert expected to hear. He was told to walk with his new best friend; they needed to see his new car. Robert turned and headed towards the front door when he felt the sharpness in is side once again. "Head to the exit through the lobby and out the side door." Once outside Robert turned towards JD and said, "What the hell do you think you're doing?" JD just told him to walk. Several blocks down the street Robert saw two, rather large, black men standing beside a Cadillac Sedan Deville, immediately he knew that he was going to take a ride. When they got a few feet away, Robert's suspensions where proven true. One of the two men opened the rear door and even offered a slight smile. JD said, "Alright asshole, get in." Robert stepped inside the back of the car and made himself comfortable. It really was not difficult; at least the knife was no longer poked in his side. Quietly, he did take a moment to check to see if he was bleeding. No. As the men got in the car, JD front passenger, one big guy driving, the other took the position in the rear next to Robert. As they pulled away from the curb JD turned around and said, "Sorry big guy, it is just we have a lot to talk about." Robert allowed a slight chuckle and simply said, "Sure." They drove for about forty-five minutes and made their way up into the hills, finally pulling into a driveway that leads to a rather impressive house. Robert guessed it was about eight thousand square feet, probably got a pool in the back he thought. As the car came to a stop, JD told Robert they would go inside and have a drink and a little talk. Again, Robert chuckled. It was clear that hearing this pissed JD off. Robert could care less. His only concern was what Tina was thinking. He was sure she was upset; after all, it had only been a few hours since they decided to live together and now he disappears. What a way to cement a relationship. This thought brought another smile to Roberts face.

Seeing this smile JD asked, "You think this is funny, I'll have that smile wiped right off your damn face!" Robert just looked at this punk, continued to smile, but choose not to laugh. The memory of the knife was still a little bit too clear. As everyone got out of the car, they all walked towards the front door, JD opened the door and everyone walked inside. Robert found a seat in a nice leather chair and when he was asked if he wanted a drink, he told them, "No thank you." JD said have it your way and he sat down in a chair across the room from Robert. He began by saying, "You seemed to take an interest in Billy. That may prove to be a real bad decision for you see that son of a bitch owes me a large sum of money and from where I sit the only reason I have not been paid lies in your lap." Robert began to speak but JD continued, "So, let me tell you how this is going to play itself out. Since you have taken it on yourself to speak for Billy, then you my friend are going to pay off his debt. I do not want to hear anything about time; I want my money now and if I do not get it, well let's just say you may be involved in a little accident." Robert could not help himself he had to chuckle again. This guy was really a punk. Just who the hell does he think he is? To Robert he was nothing more than the stuff you scrape off your shoes when you walk where a dog has recently visited.

In a low tone, Robert said, "So this is how you want to play this, is it? Well if you expect to get paid and paid soon then I need to make a phone call."

"And just who are you going to call?" asked JD. Robert told him, "I don't think it really matters who I am going to call, all you want is your money and all I want is to make sure you get it." Hearing this brought a smile to JD. He looked at Robert and told him, "Make the damn call." As Robert was dialing the number, JD was quick to tell his flunkies that this is how you get things done. After the call went through to New York

THE FINAL SCORE

Robert just hoped that the man on the other end answered. After four rings a familiar voice said, "Hello" Robert smiled and said "Don, this is Robert how are you doing?"

"I am fine my friend but things around here have been at bit unusual to say the least." Robert smiled and nodded his head saying, "I understand, listen my friend I am out in L.A. and seemed to have developed a small problem that you may be able to be of some assistance in solving." Robert new what was going to happen, when this was heard and sure enough, the laughter from the other end that could be heard through out the room. JD looked around to make sure that what he was hearing was coming from the phone. Just as he was about to say something Robert continued the conversation, "Listen my friend, this little problem has a name, it is J.D. and he is some kind of a bookie. He accepted a bet from someone I have met and was hoping to do little business with and when I explained that, it would be a week or two for this JD to get his money, well let's just say he did not like those terms. As a matter of fact he met me today and to convince me to take a ride with him he stuck a knife against my side."

"Well, well, well, Robert I would have to say you have been a bad little boy. What the hell happened to your gun?" Robert gave another chuckle and said he had it but choose not to show anything like that. This brought laughter again from the man on the other end of the conversation. After he stopped laughing he asked, "Is it safe for me to assume that I get my normal ten percent of what you're working on?"

"Of course." Robert replied. "Well then I guess I need to talk to this JD person then don't I?"

"If you don't mind I would be very appreciative!" Robert said. "Well put him on the damn phone!" the voice said.

Robert removed the phone from his ear, looking at JD said, and "It's for you?" JD looked confused by this change in events. Robert simply said, "If you wish to get what you want I would take this call." JD got up from this seat and walked over to get the phone. He placed the phone to his ear and said hello. The voice on the other end asked, "Is this JD?"

"Yes"

"It seems that you have taken a friend of mine against his will and I want you to understand that I do not like things like this happening to someone I look upon as a friend."

"Who the hell is this and why am I wasting my time talking with you? JD asked. Much to his surprise, all he heard was laughter. Finally the voice said, "I take it that Robert did not tell you who he was calling, is that right?"

"Yeah that's right."

"Well allow me this opportunity to introduce myself, I am Don Vodolchi, perhaps you have heard of me." JD thought for a minute and replied, "You expect me to believe that you are Don Vodolchi, the head of the largest crime family in all of New York, what kind of a fool do the two of you take me for?" To this the voice said, "JD I do not take you to be any type of fool, as a matter of fact I honestly believe that when we end this little conversation I know for a fact that you are going to return Robert to his hotel and make sure not to bother either him or his friend from here on out. I also know that if this does not occur as soon as possible then an associate of mind will be headed for L.A., he will then knock on your door and perform the work that he does best. In case you're wondering I am speaking of Bobby, Bobby the Steer, I am sure you have heard of him." Now JD was beginning to believe that he was really talking to Mr. Vodolchi and was not sure what to do or say. After a few moments the voice said, "I will take it from your silence that you have decided that I am who I said I am and probably have decided to do what I have asked you to do." Is correct?"

"Well I am not sure, I mean all I know is I am talking with someone on a phone that doesn't belong to me, and I am suppose to do what you say or else." JD said into the phone. "Ok, I understand that you are unsure. Why don't we do this, I will give you my phone number, look it up on the internet and you will see I am whom I say I am. Then you call me back and we will have an understanding. You do have a computer don't you?"

"Yeah I have a damn computer."

THE FINAL SCORE

"Then the only thing here JD is you need to make sure you call me back within five minutes or I call Bobby," said the voice on the phone. JD told the man that he had turned on the computer took down the number and went to work.

Looking at the computer screen JD could not believe what he was seeing. It appeared that the voice on the phone was indeed Don Vodolchi, the notorious head of the largest crime family in all of New York. He could not believe that he had just been talking to the biggest man ever associated with the mob. As he started to dial the number, he looked at Robert, god he hated that smug look on his face. After a few rings, the phone was answered and JD heard the voice saying, "Well JD I guess you have wised up in the last few minutes." JD said, "Yes sir I guess you could say that. I am sorry for not believing you the first time we spoke." Mr. Vodolchi replied, "That's nice, now about my associate Robert; is he still with you."

"Yes sir"

"Then I suggest that you give him his phone back so I may speak with him and when we have finished our conversation I will expect to hear from him, from his hotel suite. Is there going to be any problem with this JD?" JD assured Mr. Vodolchi that there would be no problem to which he was told to loose the phone number and it would be best to forget about even having this conversation. With that being understood JD handed the phone back to Robert. Robert smiled and then speaking into the phone, "Sorry I had to call you Don."

"Don't worry about it, after all this is what you pay me for." Robert laughed and agreed, and then he told Don that he would give him a call once he had gotten back to his suite.

As JD and Robert got back in the car, minus the big guys, JD started asking all kinds of questions. He wanted to know how Robert knew Mr. Vodolchi, how they had met, why would he call Robert an associate. Robert sat in silence with that smug little smile on his face. Robert knew better than to answer any of this idiots question. Yes, he had known Mr. Vodolchi for several years now, yes, he had done some work for him, and yes, he was considered an associate. However, none of this should matter to some small time bookie in Los Angles, California. No, this punk just needed to know that somehow Robert had big friends that did an excellent job of watching his back. Besides, the least JD knew the better. One thing Robert was sure about, that was he wasn't going to hear from JD again.

Stepping into the lobby of the Hilton almost seemed like being home. Now the only problem was going to be answering all the questions from Tina. As he approached the elevators, Robert heard a familiar voice calling his name. He turned to see Tina stepping out of the bar. Coming up to him Tina said, "Well nice to see you stranger, now where the hell have you been for the past two hours." Robert smiled saying, "let's go up to the room." In the elevator, all Tina did was just stand and stare. Robert hated the silent treatment but the cold stare was worse. Man, he hated feeling like this. How in the hell was he going to explain this. Entering the suite Robert headed straight to the bar. Yeah he needed a drink but more importantly, he needed to buy a few minutes too collect himself and think.

After mixing the drink he turned expecting to see Tina sitting on the couch but no such luck, she was standing less that three feet away. His first thought was why he did not sense her being so close, no idea. Tina had lost her patience by now, what with nothing been said by except "let's go to the room." Damn how she hated the thoughts that she had been having, another woman, someone for a few hours, hell she had no clue except how she felt about Robert. Nevertheless, she needed to hear the truth, no bullshit. She was the first to speak, "Listen Robert, I really care for you and all I want to know is the truth, where have you been and who have you been with." Robert sat down and looking directly into Tina's eyes he said, "Listen Tina, after you got into the elevator this damn bookie

I know came up and said he really needed to talk to me. We got in his car, I thought he was going to talk with me there but instead he drove us out to his place, up in the hills."

"Bookie, how much do you owe?" asked Tina. Robert gave a half-hearted laugh and said, "I don't owe him a penny, it was about some guy he was having trouble collecting from."

"And I'm supposed to believe that some L.A. bookie that you happen to know wanted or needed your help to get some fool to pay him off. That is what you expect me to believe." Robert took a deep breath, realizing that this was going to be tougher than he thought. "Ok Tina, I'll tell you everything I can, but you have to trust me right now some things need to be left out. The bookie met me through Billy, from The Eatery, it seems that he is into the bookie for a good amount of change and he has been attempting to stall the guy for some time. For reasons I really do not understand this clown thought I might have some influence over Billy. I explained that I really did not know him all that well but I would try to talk with him and find out what was going on. We had a drink and he brought me back here." Tina sat and listened to all of this. She had to admit that what little she knew of Robert this wild story did make a little sense. Finally, she asked, "Have you talked with Billy about this?"

"No, I tried to call him but could not find him. I told the bookie that I would keep trying, and that is the truth."

"You could have at least called me so I would not have been worrying" Tina replied. Robert smiled, "No I really could not have, I did not want to involve you in any way and besides the only person that has any idea about us is Billy and right now I wish to keep it that way." Tina nodded her head in agreement, walked over, and gave Robert a hug and kiss. This made Robert happy, his story had been believed and accepted, but the hug and kiss made him realize that this thing between the two of them was all right. He hugged and kissed her back.

With everything settled, the two decided they needed to do something about dinner. Robert called for the car and heard one would be there in thirty minutes. Hanging up and telling Tina about the car it was now time to decide where to go. Tina brought up The Eatery and when Robert objected she said, "But you like it so much." Robert nodded his head but said he would rather go somewhere else. Reaching for a phone book, Robert found the yellow pages and began looking. In the restaurant section, he found what he was looking for, The Palm. Making a note of the address, he called to make sure they could get a table. After speaking with the individual on the phone, he had a reservation at 8:30pm. He told Tina that they had just enough time to get ready and go as The Palm was about forty-five minutes from here. Tina rushed for the shower and Robert fixed himself another drink.

Tina had always heard about The Palm. Just walking in astounded her. This place was beautiful. All the tables had white tablecloths and the place settings were the finest crystal and china. The flatware was sterling silver; this was so over her head she thought. How could some girl from Vancouver, who had been in the states for about than six months find herself at The Palm. Just like Vegas, her head was spinning. Robert could sense that Tina was both excited and concerned at the same time. Placing his arm around her waist, he whispered in her ear, "You belong here, don't worry." Hearing this brought that beautiful smile to Tina's face. Her reaction was exactly what Robert had wished to see. He hoped that the evening would go without a single word about what had happened earlier today. He was not disappointed.

The ten o'clock wake call came and woke both Tina and Robert from a deep sleep. Robert headed towards the shower. The warm water brought him to a point of clearness and he realized that today was Monday, time to go to work. He needed to be in contact with Billy. He knew that once he told him about the meeting he had with JD the relief he would feel would be real. He also knew that this would farther put him into his debt and all that would do would really put Billy at ease and hopefully speed up the money. The money was all he was interested in. The only thing else that was needed was the United States government lifting the ban on air travel. Once he had the cash in his hands, he and Tina would be leaving the country. Where would they go he thought? What did it matter, he had enough money to live on for the next two lives. He had always dreamed of living a life of pure luxury, he had just never allowed himself to complete this dream by including a beautiful young woman. These thoughts brought a smile to Roberts' face damn he was happy. His only thought was would it last.

Stepping out of the shower Tina said, "I thought you were going to be in there all morning." Robert laughed and gave her a quick kiss. Pulling on a robe, he headed to the living room. He needed to make some phone calls and with Tina getting into the shower, he would have the privacy he needed. First, he called Billy and reached him at the restaurant. Billy was happy to hear from Robert and said so. Robert asked, "Will you have a few minutes to get together so we can talk?" Billy said, "Yes, mid afternoon." Robert said he would stop by as they had a lot to discuss. Billy agreed and the two ended the call with that being settled. Next, he called Mr. Vodolchi. When Don answered the phone, Robert again apologized for calling him yesterday. Don again told him not to worry about that and asked just what he had in the works. Robert told him about Billy and the problems he was having. Don wanted to make sure that this person could come up with the cash that Robert was looking for. Robert told him that he thought that Billy was going to be able to get his hands on around half a million. This brought laughter from Don. Hearing that, Robert felt so much better. Don asked if he should expect payment in the normal manner and Robert said he was not sure if he would be able to deliver it in person as he usually did. He asked Don if necessary did he have someone out here on the coast that could be used if needed. Don thought about it and finally said he knew a guy that they might be able to use. Don then asked, "Why would you use a delivery man instead of bringing it yourself?" Robert took a deep breath and said, "As soon as I can fly I am getting the hell out of the country and I don't think I will be coming back." Again, Don laughed, and then he said, "Are you telling me that you're going to retire?" Robert said that was the plan. Don's laughter was much louder upon hearing this. He really could not believe what he had just been told. No way, not Robert, hell this guy lived for the kill. It was the thrill of the chase, not the prize at the end, which made Robert so damn good at what he did. "You trying to tell me that you have had enough of all the fun and games that you have been playing for what ten years?" Don asked. Robert replied, "Hell yes, I have put enough away to live like a king, it is time to settle down just a bit." Don's laughter again was loud and he said, "Maybe I should have gotten a bigger cut." Robert laughed at this. It also pissed him off just a bit, he was paying this guy to answer the occasional phone call and politely scare the hell out of someone, a bigger cut, no way. "Yeah maybe you should have but our deal has worked well, for both of us." Robert said. "Besides, you stand to gain another fifty thousand dollars and for what a three minute phone call. Now that ain't bad now is it?" Don had to agree with that statement and said so. Before they ended the conversation, Don told Robert that if he needed or wanted to use the deliveryman to just call and it would be set up. Robert thanked him for everything and ended the call by say, "Thank you for everything and I'll be in touch."

Just as he got off the phone, Tina came walking out of the bedroom. "No coffee, you're slipping my friend." Hearing this brought a laugh from Robert. He picked up the phone and called for room service, it was the least he could do. With that done, he got up and went to the bedroom to get dressed. Stepping back into the living area, he could smell the coffee. Tina handed him a cup and asked what they were going to do today. Robert sat down and told her that he had a meeting in the early afternoon but other than that, he had nothing to do. "Well now, a meeting and then nothing." Tina said. "Must be kind of boring for you, wouldn't you say." Robert chuckled at this. Looking in her direction, without looking directly at her, he said, "I am used to having down time it's not that big of a deal." Tina smiled and told Robert she had called for a car, that she was going to stop by the Varsity to see her friends and pick up her last paycheck. Robert said that was fine and maybe they would order room service for dinner as opposed to going out. Tina said that was fine, gave him a kiss and with that she was gone.

Being alone, Robert sensed that he was a bit uncomfortable. Thinking about this feeling, he realized just how much he cared for Tina. Was it infatuation or was it something more. He was not sure what the answer was to these thoughts. Hell, he was thirty-eight years old and never felt like he had ever been in love. Was this love he wondered? All he knew was that she had been gone for a little over an hour and he missed her. What all of this meant he did not know, but he wanted to find out for sure. For the first time he realized he had a lot of acquaintances but only one true friend. He only had one person to talk with on matters of the heart, and unfortunately Denny was nowhere around. Well thinking about this was important, but he had more pressing matters that needed his attention.

It was two fifteen when he walked into The Eatery. The young lady at the hostess stand smiled and asked, "How many in your party sir?" Robert simply said he was alone and he wanted a table in the smoking section. After reaching the table, Robert took a seat with his back, as normal, to the wall and told the young lady to please let Billy know that Robert was here. She said, "I will be glad to" and with, that, she was gone. Robert had ordered a drink, and was enjoying it by the time Billy showed up.

Sitting down Billy asked Robert how he enjoyed Vegas. After hearing about the winnings that he and Tina had managed to leave with there was a tad bit of jealously that could be seen on Billy's face. After a few minutes of small talk, Robert finally asked Billy if he had heard from JD. When Billy told him that he had not Robert began telling him about the events of yesterday. Billy was relieved to hear that no one had been hurt and was more relieved when he found out that JD would not be bothering him anymore. Robert left out the information about the phone call he had made, as he knew that information did not need to be revealed. Hell, if Billy knew that Robert associated with the likes of Don Vodolchi he would probably run as fast as he could in the opposite direction than Robert was coming from. Now for the sixty four thousand dollar question.

Robert took one last sip from his drink, lit a cigarette, and looked directly into Billy's eyes and asked, "Where are you when it comes to getting the cash you spoke about?" Billy took a deep breath and said, "I should have a half of million dollars by Wednesday." Robert said that was good and asked about if he had found a way to move the product. Billy said he had found someone who convinced him that if the stuff were any good he would be able to move it in a matter of days. "That sounds great," said Robert. Keep that person to yourself; I do not need to know anything about who it is." Billy leaned closer to Robert and said, "That sounds good except for one thing."

"And what is that one thing?"

"This person said before he agreed to move the stuff he wanted to test it to make sure it is any good." Robert sat back and appeared to be giving this some thought. Finally, he sat back in his chair and said, "No problem, I'll make a phone call and set everything up. Depending on problems with travel it should not take more than a couple of days." Billy was glad to learn this. All he wanted to do was to get the stuff, make a ton of money, pay off the IRS and JD and forget about all of this crap. He went as far as to tell Robert just that. Hearing this Robert threw back his head and laughed as if he had just heard one of the funniest jokes of all time. He then looked at Billy and told him to make sure and get his cash ready and he would take care of every thing else. With that, the two men shook hands and Billy disappeared into the kitchen. Robert finished his drank, threw a few bills on the table and left.

After getting back to the Hilton Robert had to make some phone calls. First, he contacted American Airlines in an attempt to ascertain when air travel was going to be allowed to start back up. He was told that travel will be allowed on a limited base for the next few days and by the end of the week, they expected that travel would be returning to normal. Getting this information set Robert at ease with what else he had to do. The next call was to his old friend Pat in St. Louis. When Pat answered the phone, he was surprised to hear Robert on the other end. It had been several years since he had seen, let alone heard from him. After a few minutes of small talk, Pat asked Robert why he had called. Robert took a long pull on his cigarette and asked Pat, "Can you use a thousand dollars in your wallet right now?" This took Pat by surprise; giving this some thought, he finally asked, "And just what do I need to do to get that grand?" Robert gave that now famous chuckle and asked if he still could get his hands on some great powder. Pat laughed in return and immediately said, "Of course I can what else would he think." Then Robert dropped the bomb, "I need it out here in L.A. by Wednesday. Can you make it happen?" Pat had to be honest, he could get the stuff, no problem, but when it came to getting to L.A. now that presented a problem. Robert asked what the problem with making it out to the west coast. Pat was quick to tell him that right now he could not fly from ST. Louis to Kansas City on Southwest for forty-nine bucks. Again Robert laughed, he told Pat that he would call the airline and prepay the round trip ticket, no problem. With that being said, Pat told Robert he would see him in L.A. whenever the plane landed.

THE FINAL SCORE

Robert told him he would give him a call later today to let him know which airline and what time. Pat said he would be waiting on the call.

Robert was lying down on the bed when he heard the door open and close. As he lay there, he was smiling as he waited for Tina to come through the door. Much to his surprise the person that walked in was not Tina, no it was the girl from housekeeping. If one were watching this happen, it would have been difficult to tell who was more surprised. Robert jumped off the bed as the housekeeper screamed as she backed out of the room. Realizing what had happened Robert starting laughing, this did little to settle down the frightened young girl. When he stepped out of the bedroom, the housekeeper said she would come back, to which Robert said, "Nonsense. All you did was surprise me, please stay and do your job." At that exact moment, the suite door opened and Tina came rushing in. Again, the young girl screamed and simply ran out the open door. Tina stood there with a shocked look on her face and all Robert could do was laugh.

After both Tina and Robert had calmed down, he was able to explain what had happened. After hearing the whole story Tina agreed that it was funny and suggested that one of them call down to the front desk to let them know what had happened and for them to please send someone back up to clean the room. Robert said that that sounded smart and handed her the phone. After Tina made the call and was assured that someone would be up to take care of her needs she turned to Robert and asked how his day had gone. Robert told her that things could not be any better. She smiled and said that she had talked with a couple of girls at The Varsity and had spoken with the manager. She went on to tell him that the manager was less than happy that she was quitting but the two girls seemed excited to find out that Tina had a new boyfriend. Robert smiled and said, "Boyfriend, so that is what I am." Tina laughed and said, "How should I speak of you?" Robert just looked at her; he was completely dumbfounded by both what she had called him and then what she said after that. "I really have not given this much thought. To be honest I don't normally worry about what I call people, other than their name of course," said Robert. Tina looked at him in disbelief, "What do you mean, are you trying to tell me that you haven't wondered what to call me other than Tina." Robert had to be honest, "No, I really have not even thought about it." Tina shook her head as if to say I do not believe you. Finally, she asked, "What have you called your other girlfriends?" Robert gave her a little laugh and then said, "Sweetheart, you may find this hard to believe but I have never had a girlfriend before." This caught Tina totally off guard. "What do you mean; you've never really had a girlfriend before, what about when you were in school?" Robert looked at her and replied, "I realize that you may have some trouble understanding this but no I have never really had a girlfriend." Tina was in absolute shock. She wanted to believe Robert but just could not quite get her mind around the point he was trying to make. After all, he was attractive, has a good personality, had the means to show a girl a good time, what is wrong with this picture she thought. Then out of the blue, she looked at Robert and asked, "Are you gay?" Robert exploded in laughter. This was by far the funniest question he had ever been asked. After gaining control, he looked at her and said, "Have I not proven that to be false?" Tina shrugged her shoulders and said she had heard of gay men being with women to hide the fact that they were gay. Robert laughed again then said, "I am not gay, have never been gay, and do not plan on ever being gay!" Tina smiled at hearing this and then asked about school. Robert told her that he had grown up in a rural area, the closest neighbor was at least a mile away and besides, when he was in high school, he played baseball damn near year round and really did not have time for a girl friend. Yes, he dated but really not that much. Tina asked about the time since then and Robert replied that when he was working if the urge really hit him he would go out and find a wife for the night. To this, Tina wanted to know if that was all that this was or just a night for a week.

Robert took her hand in his and said, "Tina I have not quite figured out exactly how I would describe just what I feel for you but please understand and believe me when I tell you that you are not just some fling. Not for one night or one week. I am not going to sit here and tell you I know where this is going, but I want to find out where it is heading. As a matter of fact I want to be there when it gets there." Tina had to smile. She told Robert that she kind of felt the same way with one exception and that was she was beginning to think of him as her boyfriend. Robert smiled, "So, I am a boyfriend. This is a first for me and I can not think of a better person to have for this first." This caused Tina to smile again, damn she really did care for this man. She could not help but smile, hearing these words from Robert was exactly what she needed. After a few minutes she turned to Robert, still holding his hand, and after giving him a kiss she whispered in his ear, "I love you." Hearing this made Robert's heart jump and at the same time scared the hell out of him. He really did not know what to do or how to act. He smiled and gave her a kiss. The silence was awkward at best. Neither quite knew what to do. They sat there on the couch, embracing, and smiling. After a few more minutes, Robert asked if she was hungry and when she said she was, he picked up the phone to order room service. After being told that their food would be up within the hour, Robert felt relief that there was a break in the conversation. He really had not figured out how to handle the situation. He was a bit overwhelmed with what he had heard. It was not as if he did not like it, no quite the opposite, he just was not ready to say the same thing. Tina could sense the fact that Robert was uncomfortable but she was not upset. No, she was happy that she had told him what she had; after all, she meant it.

    Just as the food arrived Robert's cell phone rang. Looking at the caller id, he saw that it was form Billy. As he answered the call, he headed towards the bedroom, closing the door behind. Billy was so excited he could not stop talking. He was talking so fast that Robert could not even begin to understand what the hell he was talking about, let alone what he was saying. When he finally stopped to take a breath and Robert was able to get a word in, and that word was, "Stop." Upon hearing this Billy asked, "What the hell is your problem?" To which Robert said, "I have not understood a word you've said. Now slow done and tell me what is going on, understand." Billy apologized, took a deep breath and said, "What I was trying to tell you is that I will have my end taken care of by Thursday, Friday at the latest."

"That is excellent to hear. Are you getting the full half or what?"

"Oh no my friend I decided to shoot for the moon, in other words I guess you could say it is more like three quarters instead of a half." Hearing this was just like hearing a cash machine spitting money out. Robert could not believe his luck. Quickly he refocused on Billy saying, "Well my friend it seems like every thing is working out best for you. I must ask why the change in size?"

"Talking with the guy who said he could move the stuff, he convinced me to get as much as I possibly could as he is sure, if it is any good, he will be able to move it all and move it fast. And as you know, I really need to make this happen fast. And by the way, how fast can you set up the test?" Robert thought about this for a moment and said, "I will have to check on a few things, I'll be able to tell you that later tonight, tomorrow morning at the latest."

"That sounds great to me, just let me know when you've got it all set up and I'll take care of the rest." Billy said. Robert told Billy that he would back in touch as soon as he had things lined up. With this being said the conversation was over.

Stepping back into the living area, he saw Tina enjoying her shrimp salad. He walked over and sat down, doing his best to be nonchalant. Tina looked up and asked who was on the phone and why all the secrecy. Robert just looked at her and smiled. "Listen Robert, I am a big girl, there is no reason to protect me from whatever it is that you are into. I love you for who you are not for whatever it is you do." Robert gave this a lot of thought, he really was not sure if he should even offer an explanation as to what he did. Finally, he said, "Tina I know you're a big girl and I do not doubt for one minute that you could not handle to know what it is that I do; however, for the time being you are just going to have to trust me and not go there, alright." Tina did not like hearing this but she knew better than to push the point. With this understanding, she nodded her head and decided to let it go, for the time being anyway.

THE FINAL SCORE

Robert told Tina that he needed to make a couple of phone calls and he would be back in a few minutes. With that being said, he headed back into the bedroom closing the door behind him. His first call was to American Airlines. He was told that the first plane leaving St. Louis would be at two o'clock Tuesday afternoon, arriving in L.A. at four o'five in the afternoon. Robert said that would be fine and booked Pat on the flight. After hanging up he called Pat. Pat was happy to hear Robert's voice on the phone. Upon learning that he had a flight to L.A. the next day, he said he would be there. Then Pat asked, "How much do you need me to bring?" Robert told Pat all he needed was enough to be tested and Pat said he would have that covered. Then Robert told Pat that he would pick him up at LAX and to have a safe flight. Pat said he sure would and hung up the phone. With everything worked out it was time to have a bite to eat.

Stepping up to the table, he could not help but smile. Tina was finishing her salad and had poured herself a glass of wine. As Robert removed the cover that was designed to keep his steak warm, Tina asked he wanted a drink or a glass of wine. Robert thought for a moment and asked for a glass of red wine. Tina was more than happy to get the wine for him, hell she had be doing the same for strangers long enough it was nice to take care of Robert. He thanked her for the wine and began to cut into the steak. Placing his knife back on the table he looked at Tina and asked, "Is it safe to assume that you have a passport?" Tina said she did but it was in her safety deposit box. "Why are you asking me that, are we taking a trip?" she asked. Robert smiled and asked how Aruba sounds. Tina's eyes got the size of silver dollars and her smile was electric. Robert enjoyed seeing the fact that Tina was excited. He did enjoy making people around him happy and now doing it with and for someone he truly carried about was a bonus. He asked her if she thought she could get her passport on Tuesday. Tina said she could, all she needed was a ride to the bank. Robert told her he would call the service and make sure that she had transportation to her bank. Again, Tina smiled, her very own limo, what a trip. Then she asked, "When do you think we will be headed down there?" Robert gave this some thought and finally said he figured

Thursday or Friday at the latest. "How long are we going for?" Tina inquired. Robert smiled and said, "Does it really matter, besides, I have no ties to the states, we may spend some time just traveling."

"Just traveling, what does that mean?"

"Well let me put it this way, for sometime now all I have been trying to do is put together enough cash to live the rest of my life traveling until I found a place to settle down." Again, Tina smiled but it was obvious that she had hundreds of questions running through her mind. Robert picked up on this and told her that in due time she would understand everything, please be understanding and all your questions will have answers. Tina smiled and nodded her head, she did understand and yet no she did not. At this time, she decided to trust, which meant to trust blindly. This was something she had never done before and in doing so, she was uncomfortable. Robert leaned over to her, gave her a kiss and said, "Everything is going to fine, don't worry." As Robert was finishing the steak Tina kissed him good night and headed to the bedroom.

Robert woke about eight in the morning and the first thing he did was call the car service and tell them that Tina would be calling later today for a car and all they needed to do was add the car to his ticket and everything would be fine. Then he told them that he would need a driver within an hour. The service said they would be happy to take of her and thanked him for his business. Next, he called Billy. This was a short conversation as all he needed to do was to set up the testing. Robert told him to get in touch with his guy and take care of the arrangements. He went on to tell him that his man would be here around four so any time after that would be fine. All Billy had to do was set everything up and to let Robert know when and where. Billy said he would take of it and that he would call Robert in the early afternoon. The next phone call was to room service, he ordered coffee and the fruit bowl that Tina liked so much. At least when she got up she would have what she wanted. With all of this taken care of, he headed towards the shower.

As he got out of the shower, he noticed that Tina was awake still lying in the bed. She smiled up at him and said, "I guess you've got plans for today." Robert smiled and told her that he had a lot to take care of but she need not worry, he had taken care of getting her a car. "All you need to do is call the service and the car will be downstairs within a half an hour," Robert told her. Hearing a knock on the door, he told her breakfast is here so get up and come on out to the living area. Once Robert had a cup of coffee, he turned the television on. The first thing he saw was those damn planes flying into the World Trade Center. Damn he thought, how many times were they going to show this. Each time he saw it he became angry and this was something he did like to feel. Quickly he changed the channel. Anything was better than more bad news. When Tina came out to where he was, he told her that he would be leaving in a little while. She poured herself a cup of coffee, noticed the bowl and fruit, and smiled. She leaned over, and gave him a kiss and thanked him for the fruit. Then she said, "Well if you are leaving soon I suggest you better go get dressed." Robert chuckled and said, "Oh come on, are you saying I should not go out in this nice white robe." Tina got a laugh out of this and then said, "Ok smartass, that is enough of that!" Robert laughed and headed to the bedroom.

Stepping off the elevator Robert saw Jose waiting in the lobby. Glancing at his watch, he took note of the time. It was just past ten, he knew he had enough time to take care of all the things he needed to. As he walked up to Jose, they exchanged hellos and Robert told him he wanted to go to Tiffany's, on Rodeo Drive. Jose smiled and said they would be in just a little short of an hour. Robert gave him a questioning look and Jose said, "It is still early out here on the coast, traffic will not die down for another hour." Robert nodded his head and stepped into the Benz.

Not long after they had left the Hilton Robert's cell rang. He answered and Billy said, "How does five sound to you." Robert said that that would be fine and asked where. Billy asked if his house would be ok. Robert had to thank about this. He really did not like being at someone's house, they had all the advantages. They knew the layout, knew all the hiding places, and the quick exits. Finally, he said that it would be ok he just needed the address. Billy gave him the information and tried to give him directions. Robert interrupted him and reminded him he had a driver and felt there would not be a problem getting there. He also reminded Billy that he would be coming from LAX so if he was a bit late not to worry. Billy said that would be ok and to call if the time was getting to be much past five. Robert agreed and ended the call. He then dialed Pat's number, hoping that he would answer. Pat answered the phone on the first ring. Robert asked if everything was going as planned and he was told that it was. In fact, Pat was at the airport. Robert had forgotten about the two-hour difference in time and he had to laugh at himself. He told Pat he would see him soon and not to drink too much on the plane. Pat again told him not to worry and he would be out there in no time. They ended the conversation and Robert realized that Jose had managed to get him to Rodeo Drive a little faster than he expected.

Getting out in front of Tiffany's, Robert realized he was a little nervous. As he stepped inside, he was met with a greeting that was friendly and included his name. The woman who was speaking looked familiar but he could not remember her name. As she got closer, he was thankful to see Cheryl on her nametag. Cheryl asked what he was looking for today and Robert took a deep breath and said, "An engagement ring." Cheryl smiled, her surprise was not very well hidden, and Robert smiled back. As they walked towards a display case Cheryl asked what type of ring he was looking. Robert had to tell her he really had no idea. "This is something I have never come close to looking at before today," Robert said. Cheryl smiled and asked, "Well, would a drink or glass of wine help?" Robert thought how much that would help but wanting to keep his wits completely in place, he declined. Looking at the rings in the case, he was overwhelmed. He had never realized that there were so many different types. Finally, he looked at Cheryl and said, "I am planning on spending in the neighborhood of around ten grand; just show me what you've got. Cheryl smiled and said, "Nice neighborhood!" and pulled a tray out of the case that had five or six rings on it. Robert looked and looked. He had no idea and understanding that he asked for Cheryl to describe what a young lady would like. Cheryl took a moment to think and said, "I would recommend a marquee cut diamond set high above the actual ring. She removed one from the tray, handing it to Robert, she told him the setting was solid gold, and the diamond was two and half carats. Robert looked at the ring and knew it was the one. He told Cheryl he would take it. Cheryl asked about sizing and Robert had to admit he had no idea. Cheryl smiled and sad, "That is not a problem, after the young lady received the beautiful ring all they needed to do was come in and they could have it sized in no time at all." Robert smiled and said that would be fine. After paying for the ring and getting that special blue box, he headed back to the Benz.

Stepping back into the car, he checked his watch. It was approaching one o'clock. That was fine; it gave him enough time to grab some lunch and then head to the airport. He asked Jose if he new of any decent restaurant in the area and Jose said he new of a good Mexican place nearby. Robert said that was fine and off they went. As they pulled up to the restaurant Robert told Jose to park the car, lunch was on him. Jose smiled and found a parking spot and the two got out and went inside. After they reached their table and were seated Jose had to ask one question. "Sir, may I asked what you picked up back at Tiffany's?" Robert smiled and pulled the box out of his pocket and slide it over to him. Opening the box, Jose whistled in appreciation of what he was seeing. He asked if it was for the young lady that had accompanied Robert to Vegas. Robert again smiled and said, "What do you think?" Jose laughed and said that they made a nice couple. Robert thanked him and then said, "I hope she likes it." Jose said he felt that she would, as he did not think she was crazy. Robert nodded his head in agreement and picking up his menu said, they needed to order.

Upon leaving the restaurant, both men were satisfied and ready to continue their day. Of course, Jose had no idea what type of day Robert had planned and quite frankly, he did not care. Robert checked the time and knew they would get to LAX in plenty of time. He told Jose where they were going, Jose said that would be fine. They would be there as soon as he could manage. Robert sat back thinking about what he had bought. The more he thought about the ring, and Tina, he realized that yes he was in love. How was he going to pop the question? Man, he had no idea. This was something he had never thought about; hell, to be honest he had always figured he would spend the rest of his life alone. That thought had never really bothered him all that much. What did bother him was the mental picture of him sitting on a park bench, feeding the birds, all alone, in his old age. Well at least if she said yes that mental image would be gone, as long as she said yes. The more he thought about this the more nervous he became. As the car was pulling into LAX, he still had no idea as to how he would pop the question. The only thing he knew for sure was the he had all intentions to do so.

Stepping up to the area where people were going to disembark the American Airlines flight from St. Louis Robert hoped that Pat had done as he told him and not had too much to drink. For as long as he had known Pat, he always seemed to drink too much. As he looked up seeing people exiting the gangway, he waited to see Pat. After about half the people had come off the plane, he could see Pat making his way down the gangway. Studying carefully he breathed a sigh of relief as it appeared that Pat was sober. When Pat saw Robert, he waved and smiled. Stepping free from the crowd he approached Robert and smiled and said, "Take a breath my old friend, I only had one drink." Robert laughed and thanked Pat for taking it easy. He told him that in a couple of hours he would be on, as the test meeting was set up for about five. Upon hearing this Pat smiled as he realized that there would be time to play.

After discovering that Pat had no baggage the two made their way out of the terminal. Stepping outside Pat could no longer wait to light up a smoke. Robert smiled and did the same. Standing on the curb Pat turned to Robert and asked where he had parked. Just then, the Benz pulled up and Robert said, "Right here." This brought another smile to Pat's face. Stepping inside the car, the first thing Pat noticed was that there was no privacy divider between the front and back of the car. Getting Robert's attention and motioning to the fact that the divider was nowhere to be seen he asked if they needed to discuss anything. Robert said, "No, we can take care of that after we get to where we are going." Jose turned and asked Robert where the next stop was and Robert gave him Billy's address. Jose gave this some thought and then said, "That was fine but it will take us at least an hour and a half to get there." Robert said that was fine, and with that being stated off they went.

On the way to Billy's, Robert and Pat sat and talked. They really did not have much to say but they were able to pass the time without much effort. Robert looked at the clock on the dash it was four forty-five. He asked Jose how much more time and was told at least a half an hour. Robert reached for his cell and dialed Billy's number. When Billy answered, Robert told him they were half an hour away and unless something came up they would be there as fast as they could. Billy said all was fine, they where just having a drink and were waiting. Robert ended the conversation, turned to Pat, and said, "Play your cards right and that second drink would not be too far away." Pat smiled and said, "It's about time." This brought a laugh from both men.

Finally, Jose was pulling into a driveway. Before he stepped from the car, Robert told Jose to stay in the car, as he did not think they would be here too long. Jose said that would be fine and both men got out of the car. Walking up to the front door Robert turned to Pat and said, "When we get inside just follow my lead. I don't want to make this take any longer than it has too." Pat nodded his head and told Robert that everything was cool, in fact, he had checked the stuff before leaving St. Louis and even he was impressed. This gave reason for Robert to smile, something he had not done since buying the ring.

It did not take Billy long to open the door. After introductions and hands had been shook, Billy offered to make them each a drink. Robert said that would be nice and asked for a Crown and Coke and a vodka rocks with a twist of lime. Billy said he would have them right up and Pat smiled thinking it was amazing that Robert remembered what he preferred to drink, especially since they had not seen each other in over three years. The more he thought about this though he realized that memory was Roberts's best mental attribute, remembering this brought another smile to Pat. Billy returned with the drinks and asked if it were time to get things taken care of. Robert said that was fine but insisted they move somewhere without windows. Pat said fine and suggested his garage.

In the garage, Pat raised his shirt and removed a small, clear, bag that was been taped to his chest. All the time Robert kept looking at Billy's guy, Mike, he thought he had seen him somewhere but could not really place where. Pat handed the bag to Billy who in turn handed to Mike. Mike produced what appeared to be a test tube from his front pants pocket. Inside the tube, some clear liquid was contained with a small cork stopper. He opened the bag and removed a small sample of the cocaine and after removing the cork, he put the sample inside the tube. Replacing the cork, he gave the tube a good shake. No sooner had he stopped did the solution took on a brilliant color. Seeing this Mike whistled his approval. Billy, having no clue what was going on asked, "Is it any good?"

"Good, no it's not good, it's fantastic!" Mike exclaimed. "How fantastic?" Billy asked. Mike smiled and told Billy that this stuff could be stepped on at least once and possibly twice. This information caused Billy to literally jump up and down with glee. He knew his money problems would soon be a thing of the past. Turning to Robert, Billy asked, "When should I expect to be able to deliver?" Robert appeared to be distracted some bit and Billy asked the question again. Robert turned to Billy and replied, "When will you have the cash and how much will it be?" Billy said he should have it within the next forty-eight hours. Robert looked Billy in the eye and said, "As soon as you have the cash and I have seen it I'll make the call to have the shipment delivered."

"What do you mean you have to see the cash before arranging the damn shipment? What is the matter do you not trust me all of a sudden?" Robert sat his drink down on the hood of a car and told Billy trust had nothing to do with, but before he put his butt on the line for several kilos of coke, he was going to be absolutely sure that it would be paid for. If Billy had a problem with that, he was free to find someone else to save his butt. The tone of voice that Billy was hearing was new to him. Robert had always been civil and friendly and now he was more serious than Billy had ever seen.

Billy made a comment that that blood pressures seemed to be rising and it probably would be wise if everyone took a drink. Robert looked at Billy again and said, "My blood pressure is fine. You need to understand that this is a business, one that is run cash on demand. If that is a problem then you will just have to get over it because there would be no other way." Billy took a step back, looking at Robert he said, "Ok, Ok I get the message loud and clear." Robert smiling said, "Now that we have that cleared up there are a few things that you and I have to talk about." Billy said that that was fine and offered that they go inside, get a fresh drink, and sit down and go over it all. As everyone moved inside, Robert was not too happy about discussing the details of his operation in front of so many people but he had to admit, he had agreed to everyone being here at the same time. After getting the fresh drinks, Robert pulled Billy to the side and showed him the ring he had purchased for Tina. This caught Billy totally by surprise and all he could say was, "Wow!" Robert was please by the fact that Billy was surprised, it gave him a small opening to which he could possibly walk through. Robert closed the box and said, "Listen my friend, it is getting late, I have at least an of hour to drive back to the Hilton and I, as you can imagine, have dinner plans for tonight, so why don't we get together some time tomorrow to talk about finalizing the deal." Billy smiled and said he understood and that would be fine. Then he asked where dinner was going to take place. Robert said he was not sure but he would make a reservation during the ride back. Billy would have nothing of that, no he insisted that they dine at The Eatery and he would make sure everything was perfect. Hell, the night would be on him. Robert smiled and said that was very kind and Billy said it was the least he could do. With everything be settled they shook hands knowing they would be seeing each other in a few hours. Robert and Pat made their way out to the car.

In the car, Pat asked where he was staying. Robert told him he had a room for him at the Hilton and would provide transportation to the airport tomorrow. Pat was appreciative but it did not take long for him to get around to asking about the grand that he was supposed to get for this little job. Robert smiled and told him to come up to his suite after he was settled in his room and he would take care of it. Pat agreed and the two sat in silence for the remainder of the ride.

As Robert stepped inside his suite the first thing he saw a box from FedEx. He smiled with the knowledge that his cash had arrived. Before he could make his way to the box Tina stepped around the corner and he could see that she was full of questions. He gave her a kiss and headed to the bar; damn he really needed a drink. What with everything that had gone on at Billy's house, the ring in his pocket, dinner, the question, the damn question. He still had no idea how he was going to ask Tina to marry him. Hell, he had not even told her that he loved her. Tina's first question brought him back to the moment, "What is in the box Robert?" He turned in hopes of being able to deflect the question but the look in her eyes told otherwise. Smiling he said, "It's nothing, just something from a friend of mine in Aruba."

"Some friend, I wish I had a friend that would send me a box full of cash." Robert head snapped around as if it were on a pivot. "You opened the damn box!" Robert exclaimed. Tina was shocked by his response and said, "Yeah, no one told me not to open the damn box. Matter of fact no one told me a damn box was even coming. So back off my ass will you." Robert took a step back, collected his thoughts and said, "Sweetheart, I sorry. I did not mean to snap at you. It has been a rather unusual day and everything here just caught me by surprise." Tina relaxed hearing sweetheart, but was still extremely curious about what she had seen in the box. Again she asked, "If you don't mind could you please explain a box from Aruba filled with money and who it came it from." Robert smiled and said, "Ok I guess it is time to answer those twenty questions that have been running around that pretty head of yours. Why don't I fix you a drink and we can sit down and discuss everything." Tina said that would be fine and Robert headed to the bar and pored her drink.

Sitting down on the couch Robert took a deep breath and lit a cigarette. Tina was waiting patiently but the suspense was enough to stop a runaway freight train. Finally Robert spoke, "The box is from my banker in Aruba, I called him a few days ago and wanted him to wire the money to me but because of those damn terrorist attacks in New York it was impossible to get the wire through. He suggested the FedEx shipment. The money is from my account down there. I meant to tell you that it may be here today but with everything I had on my mind this morning I forgot." This explained the money and the box but Tina still had so many questions. Before Robert could continue speaking Tina asked, "Will you please tell me where the money came from?" Robert smiled and told her he just had. The money was from his banker in Aruba. "No.," Tina said, "I mean how did you get that kind of money to begin with?" Robert took a long drag on his smoke and a large drink from his glass. Again before he could speak Tina said, "Listen, you know I love you, just tell me the truth and it will be fine." Robert smiled, leaned forward and said, "Tina, you once asked me what I was doing out here in L.A."

"Yeah you told me you were in sales" Tina interrupted. Robert chuckled, "Yes that is what I told you. It was the truth, in a way."

"The truth in a way, what the hell does that mean?" Tina asked. Robert asked for a minute, he was trying to explain everything to her. "What I sell is hope, dreams, a mirage if you will. Some would call me a con man. I prefer salesman."

"How does someone sell hope and dreams?" Tina asked. Robert smiled, "It is really quite easy. All one has to do is find someone who needs help, big help, and show them there is a solution to their problem if they are willing to take a risk."

"What kind of risk?" Tina wanted to know. "Tina, I find people who need to turn their money into so much more. I tell them that for the right price I know people who can help. All they need to do is invest in as much cocaine as they can afford, sell it, and whalla, money problems are gone."

"Oh my God, you're a dope dealer," a shaken Tina cried. Robert raised his hand in an attempt to get Tina to calm down. Her concern was clearly etched across her face. Robert could see and feel her pain damn he hated this. "Tina I am not a dope dealer. In fact, I hate people that sell drugs. No, as I said, I sell hope and dreams, it's just that the hope never arrives and dreams turn into nightmares." Robert attempted to explain. "You see they give me the cash and what they think they're buying never shows up. All they get are broken promises and out right lies." Tina sat trying to grasp all of this. What she was being told seemed so unreal. The man that she fell in love with is a liar and a cheat. No, that is not who he is, she thought. This man was nice, real, and thoughtful, there was no way he could be what he was trying to tell her. Finally Tina was able to shake the fog out of her mind and asked, "And what, these people that you con don't get mad or try to get their money back" Robert laughed when he heard this question, "Mad no, pissed hell yes. Do they want their money back, bet your ass they do; however, the way I set the deal up, we both are ripped off so we both lose. You see, the cash and the drugs are never in the same place, and low and behold, the man with the drugs never shows up. No he ripped us both off or he was busted or some other line of bullshit. The one thing you have to understand is the people are so desperate they will believe just about anything. Hell, there have been a few times I have ripped the same person off more than once. Remember, they are desperate."

"What stops them from going to the police?" Tina asked. Again Robert laughed, "Oh yeah that would really work. Let's see, gee mister policeman, I was trying to buy a large quantity of cocaine and the person who was selling it ripped me off. Yeah that would do them a ton of good." Tina was starting to get the picture. She was beginning to understand what she was hearing. Robert looked into her eyes and asked, "Have I answered all your questions?" All Tina could do was shake her head.

The two sat and talked for about an hour. Robert did his best to answer all of Tina's questions. He held nothing back, each question received its answer and finally Tina appeared to be relaxed and comfortable again. With a full understanding of what Robert had told her, she asked, "And who is the dreamer this time?" Robert wanted to know if she really wanted to know and Tina did her best to convince him that she did. Realizing that she really did want to know, Robert spoke one word, "Billy."

"Billy, you have to be kidding. I mean that man has it all, a nice house, a nice car, and a successful restaurant. Why does he need to get his hands on the type of cash your talking about" Tina responded. Again Robert laughed, "Oh he's got problems alright. He owes the IRS and a bookie a lot of money."

"Damn I would have never guessed. He always seemed, so together, you know" Tina finally said. To which Robert replied, "It is always like that, you meet the mark and he seems together and successful, but behind the façade is the underbelly of a troubled fool. The person that is in over their head, and have no idea how they got there let alone how to get back. They are so quick to jump at the chance to wipe everything away in one fell swoop. It just goes to show you how stupid they are."

Robert was surprised that telling all of this to Tina had not scared her off. Honestly, he was impressed damn she was tough. Sitting on the couch, he could feel the Tiffany's box in his pocket. Having told her everything, he could not wait to pop the question, but wait he must. He wanted everything to be perfect. The only problem was he had no idea what perfect meant, let alone what it was. Suddenly there was a knock on the door. Robert immediately knew it was Pat wanting his damn money. Oh how much he hated giving money to away, but he had to admit to himself, it proved to be money well spent. Opening the door Pat stepped in, looking around he spotted Tina's shoes. "Sorry man, I did not mean to interrupt anything," he said. Robert smiled and told Pat that he was not interrupting anything. Having said that he handed Pat an envelope that contained the cash. Pat took a quick look inside, smiled and said he was out of here. Robert told him to give him a call in the morning and he would get him a car to take him to LAX. Pat said he would and with that, he was gone.

Robert stepped into the bedroom to see Tina lying on the bed. Looking up at him Tina asked who was at the door. Robert told her, "It was just someone who did me a favor, and not to worry about it. Besides, we have a dinner date." This brought a smile to Tina and she jumped up and gave him a nice hug. "You do understand that I love you Robert. Don't you?" Robert smiled and told her he did, he just could not yet say the same. He wanted to but the words just would not come out. Damn, this was a lot tougher than he thought.

THE FINAL SCORE

As Tina and Robert stepped through the revolving door at the Hilton, they saw Jose just up the street. Jose waved and smiled as the two approached. Naturally, he had the passenger door open before they even arrived. As she was getting in the car Tina asked, "And where are we dining my dear?"

"The Eatery" Robert mouthed. "Oh my God, I can not believe that we are going there with everything you are doing" Tina laughed. "That is the exact reason we are dining there. He invited us and the last thing I would want to do is upset him in anyway." Robert told her. "You are a bad man." Tina said through a mischievous grin. All Robert could do at this time was laugh. "You really have no idea just how bad!" he said. This brought a big laugh from Tina.

After stepping out of the car, Tina grabbed Robert's arm and gave him a big hug. "What was that for?" asked Robert. Tina smiled and said, "That was for being so honest with me tonight. At least now I think I'm truly getting to know the man that I have fallen in love with." Robert smiled, damn this girl really knows how to make me happy, I just hope it last, he thought. Stepping inside they were greeted by Billy. He was truly happy to see both of them and could not wait to express this happiness. Robert thought that this behavior was just a bit over the top. Damn, this idiot had better not spoil his surprise. Billy escorted them to their table and asked if they would care for a drink. As Robert and Tina discussed this Billy waited impatiently, all he wanted to do was bring out the bottle of champagne he had been chilling for the past hour. Finally, they decided to have a glass of wine and with that, Billy was gone.

"Don't you think he was acting a little unusual?" asked Tina. Robert nodded and said that maybe he had been hitting the sauce just a little. After all, he had had a pretty good afternoon. This brought laughter to both of them. Tina kind of liked being in on the bad stuff, she found it exciting in a strange sense. Billy returned with their wine and a platter of Calamari. As he set the platter down he smiled and said, "I remember how much you two liked this the last time yall were in and I just figured it would be a nice way to start things off. Robert and Tina both thanked

Billy and asked that he give them some time to look at the menu. Robert got Billy's attention and flashed ten fingers at him, hoping he would pick up on the fact that he wanted at least ten minutes alone. Billy smiled and said he would give them as much time as they needed.

    Robert sat there just looking a Tina. Each time she looked in his direction all he could do was smile. Finally, Tina said, "What?" Robert realized it was now or never. He took her hand in his and, with a little smile, looking into her eyes. "Tina, ever since I met you I have come to understand just how unhappy I have been. Spending time with you, going to Vegas, having you living with me has been both relaxing and comforting. This is new to me but I totally believe that I too have fallen in love. And before you make one of your smartass comments I want you to know that you are the person that I have fallen in love with." All Tina could do was smile. This was more surprising than what he had told her back at the suite. It was what she had been longing to hear but she really did not think that it would happen this fast. Damn, she really did care for this man. What happened next was even more surprising. "Tina I have something I would like to ask you. Is there anyway that you would consider spending the rest of life with me?" Robert said. You could have knocked her over with a feather. Looking at Robert in almost disbelief she asked, "What are you asking exactly?" Robert pulled the box out of his pocket and placed it on the table. Slowly he opened the box and pushed to her saying, "Tina, will you marry me." Tina tried to take a breath but no air entered her lungs. Between hearing the question and seeing one of the most beautiful diamond rings she had ever seen. To say she was breathless would be an under statement. Her head seemed to be spinning as if it were a top. The next thing she realized tears were running down her cheeks. She could not focus on anything, in fact her eyes kept moving from the ring to Robert's eyes and back to the ring. Robert said, "Damn if I would have known this was the way to shut you up I might have asked that question several days ago." Tina laughed which was a good thing. Her laughter brought her back to near consciousness. Wiping the tears from her cheeks she looked into Robert's eyes, smiling she said, "Oh yes, you can bet your ass I will marry you."

The dinner, champagne, and time passed with little attention paid to the details. Tina was beside herself with excitement and Robert with as sense of happiness yet lacking in self-confidence. The only person he had ever committed himself to was Robert. And yet, as he sat here the happiness he felt was something very new to him. He was pleased with his decision to ask Tina to marry him. He new that he had come clean with her earlier, allowing her to know the true him and he only hoped that she not only understood but would be able to accept what he had told her. He decided to let these thoughts pass; after all, it was too important of a night.

Upon getting back to the suite, they found a bottle of champagne, chilled and waiting for them. Tina thought that Robert had set this up while Robert had no idea where or from whom it had come from. Tina rushed to open the bottle and Robert decided to let sleeping dogs lie for the time. They enjoyed the champagne while listening to soft music. It did not take long for the champagne to remove any inhibitions that Tina might have been feeling and Robert suggested they move to the bedroom.

Robert awoke around ten and quickly found himself in the living area trying to track down who had sent the champagne last night. Calling room service was absolutely no help. All they could say was it was ordered around nine thirty and was delivered at ten. He was told the form of payment was cash. Now he really had no idea and he really was not comfortable. The only people that knew that an engagement was forthcoming were Jose and Billy. He felt fairly comfortable that neither of those two had been so kind. But who? Robert thought. Damn I have to figure this out, people are not supposed to know what I am doing, especially in my private life. Robert made a promise to himself that he had to find the answer to this question. Being unsure of anything was not an area that he had spent much time in and he swore he would not be there for long. With these thoughts totally encompassing his mind he did not notice that Tina had come from the bedroom.

"Well, you are the early riser today." Tina said smiling as she could not help herself from staring at the beautiful ring she now wore. She gave Robert a kiss and asked if coffee was on its way up. Robert could not help but laugh and had to admit that he had not ordered any, but he would. Reaching for the phone, she looked at Robert and said, "No bother, I'll take care of it." This brought a smile to Robert; I can get use to this he thought. Soon after the coffee and fruit arrived, Robert told Tina he needed to leave to take care of a few things and would be back later during the afternoon. Tina simply smiled; all of her attention was on the ring.

Robert called the call service and headed for a shower. By the time he got down to the lobby, Jose was waiting outside. Robert stepped in the car and with no idea of where he was going, he told Jose just drive. He had so much going on in his head. He wondered when Billy would have the cash. He wondered if he and Tina would have any problems making it to Aruba. He wondered how long they would stay there and where they would go next. Damn I have to clear my head, Robert thought. Looking out the window as they made their way north to Palm Springs, Robert asked Jose if his friend made it to the airport this morning. Jose replied, "Boss, I picked him up but we did not go to the airport. No sir, he had me drop him off at the Staples Center." Robert thought for a moment and told Jose to turn the car around. As they made their way back towards L.A. Robert called the suite several times with no luck. He tried Tina's cell and again no luck. He began to worry. Where in the hell is she and why is she not answering her damn cell, thought Robert. This was new. Tina, during the time that they had been together had never been out of touch. Damn, he was concerned, no to be honest, he was worried. He could not wait until he got back to the Hilton.

Back at the Hilton Robert could not get to the suite fast enough. As he walked through the door, he called out for Tina. No response. He began looking around for her throughout the suite. No one there. He flipped open his cell and punched her number in again, still no answer. Walking back to the living room, he noticed a piece of paper on the coffee table. Picking it up and reading what was written the blood-drained form Robert's face.

She is not here, no she is with me.
If you want to see her again
Meet me downstairs in the bar.
Billy

What the hell is going on, Robert thought. Making his way to the elevator, he reached to feel his gun. He had left it in the suite. Returning to the suite, Robert went straight to the bar. Reaching behind the bottles, he felt his shoulder holster and picked it up. Damn, it seemed light, he thought. No gun. What the hell.

Returning to the elevator, he was shaken and pissed. Robert was trying to get a grasp on just what was going on. Obviously, Billy has escalated the situation. Stepping out of the elevator, the first person he saw was Pat. This was the last person he expected to see. And to make matters worse he was smiling. As Robert turned the corner to reach the bar, he saw Billy sitting at a table, alone. Robert walked over and sat down. Billy asked, "May I get you a drink?"

"Hell no, where the hell is Tina?" Robert replied. "Slow down big guy, what is the rush? Tina is safe, and will remain that way, as long as you play fair. I do not want her; all I want is for you to follow through on all your promises. Of course, there will be a few changes. From this day on, I am in charge. We do things my way or, what was it you said the other day, oh yeah, or the highway." Billy said. Robert sat there unsure of what to say let alone to think. This was definitely virgin ground. Ground he never thought he would ever have to set foot on. Sure, there had been a few times that he had a gun to his head or a knife to his throat, but this involved someone other than him. "Just what is it that you want me to do?" asked Robert. "You need to get the damn shit out here and in my hands as fast as you can. Once it is in my control, and only when it is in my control, will any monies be handed over. Then and only then will you see your fiancée again. Now is that clear enough for you or do I need to draw you a picture?" Billy said. "I have already told you that I can't get the shit out here until I have seen the cash," replied Robert. "Well, as I just told you, you are no longer in control, I am. You will see the cash when I see the shit." Billy said. Robert stood to leave and turned looking at Billy said, "I'm telling you one thing right now, you think your in charge, fine, but if one hair on Tina's head is hurt in anyway"

"What I am a dead man?" Billy interrupted. "Oh no, your not just dead, no you will be begging for death." Robert finished. With that being said, Robert left the bar. Stepping into the lobby he again saw Pat. Walking over to Pat Robert said, "You think you're so smart. You will rue the day we ever met my friend, and you can trust me on that. And have I ever lied to you?" Robert said. Pat just looked at him. Watching Robert make his way to the elevator Pat knew enough to know that Robert did not make false threats. For the first time since Billy came to his hotel room last night, he was beginning to think that this might not have been such a good idea. Granted, being promised twenty five thousand sounded good but crossing Robert was probably a mistake. This was true, especially when you take into account the people that he knows.

Billy walked up to Pat and said, "You don't look so good my friend."

"I'm fine, you just better be sure that you know what you're doing. 'Cause if you don't, there is the possibility that we may have bitten off a little bit more than we can chew." Pat replied. "Don't worry; I know exactly what I am doing. This is certainly not the first time I have taken a risk," said Billy. "I know that is what you claim; I just hope you're right," replied Pat.

Walking back into the suite Robert went to the bar and poured a stiff drink. After taking the first swallow, he threw the glass across the room. The first thought that went through his mind was he needed to stay clearheaded right now; do not need to be drinking. This is real; this is not a con game. No, he needed to keep his mind clear so he could think this one through. Robert knew he could not get his hands on the drugs that Billy was expecting. He also knew that Tina would be in real trouble if he did not come up with something and fast. Whom did he know, who could help. Reaching for his cell, he dialed the number.

Don Vodolchi answered his phone on the third ring, as usual. Robert began telling him of the events of today. Don interrupted him when Robert said my fiancée has been kidnapped. "Fiancée, what the hell are you talking about?" inquired Don. Robert explained that he had met this girl a week ago Monday and things had been just too good. "Does she know this Billy?" asked Don. "Yeah they know each other. Why?" asked Robert. "Is there any chance that she is in on this whole thing? I mean could she have been playing you my friend."

"No. If she is, then she is better at running a scam than I am. I do not see that as being possible. I am sure that she is innocent in all of this. I mean the only thing she has done wrong here is getting involved with me." Robert stated. "Ok then, let me make sure I am completely up to speed on this. You had set everything up just as you normally do. You had Billy believing that you were his most believable help. He was willing to risk whatever cash he could raise in hopes of being able to pay everybody off. You had made sure that he looked upon you as a friend, and therefore trusted you and even relied on you. Is all of this right?"

"Yes, just like I have done at least a hundred times before" Robert said. "Ok, is there anything that you have done that is different?"

"No, each step of the way has been the same. Hell, when he told me I needed to provide a test, I used the same guy for St. Louis that I have used in the past."

"But did you not tell me that he is in on this."

"Yeah that is right. However, I am sure he is only trying to be paid. The son-of-a-bitch must have promised him a lot to get him to cross me." The two talked for a few more minutes and then Don told Robert he would look into seeing what he could do to help and would be back in touch soon. Robert thanked Don and the conversation was over.

All Robert could do at this time was pace the room. He would turn the television on and off just as fast. He would go to the bar but not pour a drink. He would turn on the sound system but no music seemed to calm him down. Nothing he did seemed to be of any help. He had not felt so helpless since watching his father battle cancer. He was young, sixteen, when it all began, but he remembered it well. A drunk driver had killed his mother when he was three but this was different. He watched his father go from a big strong man to a point that he could not hold a plastic cup to get a drink of water. He once thought that was hell, but now he felt he had found something worse. He hated to admit it, but going through this only proved that what he thought was love actually was love indeed. He looked at his watch to see it six o'clock in the evening. He knew he needed to eat but he was not hungry one iota. Finally, he called room service and ordered some nachos and a margarita. Hell, he figured, even if the nachos sucked, he probably would enjoy the drink.

After nibbling on the chips and finishing the drink, he again looked at his watch, seven-thirty. Damn time was not moving. When would Don call back. Would Don call back? Robert knew he was the only one who could help. But what kind of help, now that was an interesting thought. Don, much like Robert, hated drugs and the people who sold them, more than any other thing that walked on the earth. Robert could no longer think about all of this. He headed to the bar and again poured a stiff drink. This time he did not throw the glass. After several of these stiff drinks, he fell asleep on the couch.

The pounding on the door was enough to wake the dead. Robert rolled off the couch in a deep fog. He walked to the door and asked who was there. The only thing he heard was more knocking. Opening the door, he could not believe his eyes. In front of him stood a short, stocky, dark haired man he had not seen in several years, Bobby the Steer was standing in front of him. Robert said good morning and pushed the door all the way open and stepped back to allow the Steer to come in. After the two had grabbed seats in the living area, the Steer looked around and said, "Nice room pal." Robert chuckled at hearing this. "What brings you to the west coast Bobby?" asked Robert. The man sitting across the room from him simply said, "Mr. Vodolchi asked me to come out here to check on you. He seemed a bit worried. It has been a long time since I have seen that in him. I do not think you have any idea how much that man cares about you. In addition, when he heard that you, of all people, had gone and gotten yourself engaged he said he had to do something. So here I am." The two men sat and discussed the events of the last twenty-four hours. Robert told Bobby everything that he could think of that might be important. Finally, the Steer looked at Robert and said, "I am just out here to make sure you're alright. Mr. Vodolchi will be here tonight."

"What, Don is coming out here? Damn that is the last thing I would have expected."

"Like I said, I don't think you have any idea how much that man cares about you. Hell, he was sick when he got off the phone with you last night.

At first, he wanted me to come out here with some guys I have worked with before and just kill everyone, but then he decided against it. You know Mr. Vodolchi, sometimes he thinks it is still the fifties and you can just go around shooting the place up" This bit of information gave rise to a laugh from Robert. "Have you heard anything from this punk Billy?"

"No, not since I saw him downstairs in the bar yesterday."

"Ok, are you using our car service?"

"Of course."

"Fine, you give them a call and get me a car, I am going to go to the punks place for lunch."

"What the hell are you going there for?"

"Don't worry yourself; I just want to get a read on this guy. You know, just in case." Robert smiled. He knew or at least thought he knew what that meant. After all, the man sitting across from him is reported to have killed twenty-six people over the past fifteen years. For all Robert knew number twenty-seven would be over lunch. Robert looked at the wall clock that showed it was ten in the morning. Realizing that Bobby was on east coast time, in other words to him it felt like one in the afternoon, so he offered him a drink. Bobby said that would be nice since he would not be at the punks' restaurant for a few hours. Robert fixed him what he remembered he drank, scotch and soda. Handing it to him brought a brief smile to Bobby's face. A brief smile is all anyone ever got out of Bobby. After taking a big slug out of the drink Bobby asked, "What can you tell me about this guy from St. Louis?" Robert gave this some thought and then replied, "He is real small time. I have known him for about twelve years and all he does is try to find ways to cash in. I am sure that is all that he's doing now." Bobby thought about this for a brief moment and then said, "Maybe he will be first." Robert knew exactly what that meant and he had to say that would be fine with him. He believed that if it were not for Pat none of this would be happening. He could only wonder what he had told Billy. Well he could not worry about that now. No his only concern was with Tina.

Every time he thought of her, he could not help but worry about what she must be going through. He could only imagine what must be going through that pretty little head of hers. Damn, he missed her and he wanted her back. Robert got up to go to the bedroom; he felt a shower would go a long way in making him feel better. Remembering that Bobby had said he needed a car, he stopped and called the service. After hanging up the phone, he told Bobby his car would be here in thirty minutes and with that, he was headed to the shower.

After he was dressed, he went out to the living area to discover that Bobby was gone. Now all he could do was sit and wait. Damn if there was anything he hated this was it. For all the time that he had waited on marks to come up with the cash, that did not bother him. No, in times like that he knew his reward was coming. Now, he did not know. All he could do was hope. Billy was right, he no longer was in control and he really did not like this at all. It was not like he was some kind of a control freak it was just he had always been able to stay at least one-step ahead of whoever he was working. Even when he was threatened, he never felt he was in any real trouble. He had always been able to talk himself out of just about anything. Damn he thought, I really need to catch my snap. He grabbed a pack of smokes only to discover he had only one left. With that, he headed for elevator; there was no way he could get through all of this without smokes. Stepping outside, the fresh air felt good. Robert did not mind the three block walk to the closest convenience store. No the walk was helping to clear his head.

Back in the suite, he sat in silence, and the silence was driving him crazy. He turned the stereo system on, anything was better than silence. Damn he missed Tina and all of her silly questions. He got up and fixed a drink, turned off the stereo and turned on the television. Looking at the screen, it was more about the damn terrorist attacks. Damn, he thought, it has been ten days and this was all that anybody seemed to be talking about. At least baseball would be starting back tonight and football soon. Anything would be better than all of the pundits telling what they thought caused the attacks. Hell Robert thought, the people behind the attacks hate us, what more is there to talk about. He turned off the set and fixed another drink. It was only one-thirty; don't need to get drunk, that was for damn sure. He lay down on the couch and closed his eyes.

Hearing the door open Robert jumped from the couch. He had forgotten that he had given Bobby a key. Bobby walked in, went over to the bar and poured a drink. Robert looked at the clock, three-forty-five, where had he been for the last four plus hours, Robert thought. Finally Bobby spoke, "I have to tell you, that Billy guy is a real clown. Moving around his place and talking with people as if he is a real big shot. If that idiot were in New York, he would be laughed out of town. Anyway, after lunch I had your driver, Jose, run me out to his house. I think that is where they are holding your woman. I saw a couple of black guy walking around outside. Those two were fairly large guys, would hate to tangle with them in a dark alley." Robert knew these guys; they were probably the two that Billy had with him the he forced him to take a ride. "How do you think we should handle things now?" asked Robert. Bobby just shook his head and said, "We don't, I spoke with Don and he will be here tonight." With that being said, the Steer got up and headed towards the bedroom, "I going to take a nap." And with being said, he closed the door behind himself.

Tina wished she knew what was going on. Where was Robert? She thought. All she knew was that yesterday, after Robert had left; Billy had knocked on the door and told her he was sent to pick her up. The next thing she knew was she was in a strange house and was told that she could make no phone calls. She had not slept last night and she was really tired and simply running on raw emotion. Damn, she wished she knew what the hell was going on. Was Robert all right, did he know where she was; would he be coming to get her like a white knight on his trusted steed? Damn all she wanted were answers to her questions. Hell, someone to ask these damn questions to would be nice.

She heard the lock on the bedroom door open and in walked Billy. Just as yesterday, he still had that stupid grin on his face. God, how she hated that look. Billy looked at her and said, "I trust you have been ok today." Tina nodded her head, talking to this asshole was out of the question. "Can I get you anything? Billy asked. "Yeah you can get my fiancée over here to take me home." Tina replied. "Take you home, what the hell are you talking about, you two are staying in a suite at the damn Hilton. You don't have a home and doubt your precious fiancée has a home to take you to you stupid bitch." Oh how Tina hated that word. How this asshole dare call me a bitch, she thought. Just wait until Robert gets here because there sure will be hell to pay.

Finally Tina figured what the hell, might as well try to find out what is going on. "Billy, why are you holding me here? She asked. No response.

"What the hell is going on, I thought you and Robert were friends. Is this how you treat your friends' fiancée?" Again no response. As Billy went to the door, he turned and asked, "I am going back to the restaurant, can I get you anything?"

"Yeah, Robert!" Tina screamed. All Billy did was open the door and laugh. Closing the door behind him, Tina heard the lock go into place. Damn she never really liked that guy and now she found herself hating him.

Tina's frustration only grew more and more. She had no clue why she was here, nor what was going on. She believed that by now, Robert knew what was going on and all she could do was hope that he knew how to get to her. If anyone could, surely it was Robert. As she thought about things she knew that the reason she had been taken had to have something to do with what Robert was attempting to do with, rather to, Billy. But what could have gone wrong. Robert had told her he had Billy right where he wanted him. He had gone as far as to say that everything was exactly where it was supposed to be. It would be only a few more days they would be heading to Aruba. Something obviously had gone wrong, but what.

All Robert could do was wait. He knew that Don was on his way out here but when would he arrive. Moreover, what was he planning? Damn, not knowing was going to drive him crazy, he thought. Looking at the clock showing the time to be seven-thirty, Robert hoped that Don got to L.A. soon. At least then, they could formulate a plan of attack. No sooner had that thought passed through his mind a knock on the door made him jump. Robert went to the door, and opening it, he saw Don. Standing six feet tall, wearing his famous Armante suit and alligator shoes he did look damper. As he walked in, he grabbed Robert by the shoulders and kissed him on each cheek. The two men embraced and upon breaking the hug Don asked, "How you doing son?' Robert smiled and said, "I guess the best I can."

"Well would it be too much for an old man to get a drink?" Again Robert smiled and replied, "No trouble at all my friend, what would you like?"

"How about a good scotch?" Robert smiled and headed towards the bar. After pouring a glass of Pinch, he returned to the living area and handed the glass to Don. Don took a sip, smiled, and asked where Bobby was. Robert told him that he was in the bedroom taking a nap. Don could not help but laugh at this and then said, "Well let's let him sleep, we have some things to talk about." Hearing this Robert felt at ease, it appeared that his New York friend might just have a plan.

Don had almost finished his scotch before he spoke. "Do we know where she is?"

"Yes, Bobby thinks she is being held at the guys' house."

"And how did he come to this conclusion?"

"He had my driver take him out there this afternoon. He told me that there were a couple a large, black guys that seemed to be guarding the place, and based on that we both agreed that that must be where she is being held."

"Ok, so we think we know where she is, did he offer any ideas on what needed to be done to get her out of there?"

"No he didn't and I did not ask."

"Let's back up a minute. Who is this girl and how did you meet her?"

"Her name is Tina; she is from Vancouver, British Columbia. I met her at a local sports bar she was my waitress. She is very smart, beautiful, and very caring. We just started talking and one thing led to another. You know how it goes, boy meets girl, boy likes girl, girl likes boy, they have dinner and a few days later they're living together." Hearing Robert describe his relationship with Tina in this manner caused him to shake his head and laugh. "This all sounds like fun but are you sure she is the one?"

"Honestly, I was not sure if being told what I have done, the people I have taken from, the way I have made my fortune would scare her off. Instead, she listened and accepted. So I must state that, yes sir I am sure she is the one." This brought a large smile to Don's face. Again, he grabbed Robert by the shoulders and kissed him on both checks to show his approval.

At this time, the bedroom door opened and Bobby came walking out saying, "I thought I heard your voice." Don turned saying, "Well hello sleepy head, glad to see you." The two men shook hands and all three sat down and began to talk. "So Bobby, I understand that you thank you know where this girl is being held."

"Yeah I think so."

"Can we just go in and get her?' "No I don't think that would be wise. Not knowing the complete layout of the house or where she is actually is in the damn house, if we go in, there is no guarantee that she will live though the move."

"Well we surely don't want anything happening to her do we Robert."

"I would rather not have anything happen to her.," replied Robert. "Ok, it looks like Bobby has at least done some ground work, now all we need to do is come up with a plan that will work and also allow us to win." Robert sat and shook his head, he felt that he had thought of everything and could not come up with any idea that allowed anybody but Billy to win.

Looking at Don all Robert could do was think that he already had an idea. "What is on your mind Don?" Don stood up and went to the bar. After fixing another scotch he returned to his chair and asked, "Robert how much cash do you have on you right now?"

"On me I would have to about twenty grand, but I do have another two hundred in the hotel safe."

"Two hundred dollars in the hotel safe, who were you trying to impress." smirked Don. "Two hundred grand, thank you." Robert fired back. "Besides why do you want to know my cash situation?"

"Well, there is always the possibility of simply buying her back," said Don. "Buying her back, I thought you said we should find a way to get this situation settle that was a win."

"Ok, are you sure that buying her back is something you would rather not do."

"Hell yes, the last thing I want to do is give this son-of-a-bitch the cash he needs. No way, I would rather rot in hell than do anything remotely like that." Robert firmly said. "Well then, I guess I need to find a pay phone, in a quiet area so I can try to set something else up. And by the way, Robert, if I go this route it is going to cost you. Before you pitch a fit understand that you will still stand to get the asshole's cash."

Robert smiled; he liked what he was hearing. "This is starting to sound better by the minute." Robert said still smiling.

"Well with that agreed on I just have one more question," said Don. Robert looked at Bobby who was looking at him and simply shrugged his shoulders. "Ok and what might that be?" asked Robert. "Is there a decent Italian restaurant anywhere around here?" Robert laughed and had to say he had no idea but he could find out. With that being said, he picked up the phone and called the car service, asking the question and hoping that the answer would not be a disappointment to Don, he waited. Hanging up the phone, he said his driver would be downstairs within a half an hour and Italian cuisine would be the meal of the night.

Before they arrived at the restaurant Robert knew that if this place were good the night would go into the wee hours of the morning. Italians made dinner into an event. Multiple courses, bottles of wines and conversations about the good ole days, yes he could hope.

Getting out of the car all three men looked up and smiled. The name of the place was Distefano's; at least the named seemed authentic. Stepping inside it was immediate; the smells told each of the men that they had found the right place. After getting to their table, Don disappeared. In a few minutes, he was back with a huge smile on his face. It did not take him long to let it be known that he had met the owner and they would soon have the place to themselves. Just like New York, these three men felt at home.

Tina found herself still locked in the bedroom. She had no idea what time it was but by looking outside she knew it was night. She was hungry and tired. She really did not know which problem bothered her the most, but the idea of food did sound good. Banging on the door as loud as she could, she only hoped someone would come and check on her. After a few minutes of banging, until her hand hurt, she heard the lock open. The door was pushed open, almost knocking her down, and one of the black men wanted to know what the problem was. "A little something to eat would be nice." He stared at her as if she was insignificant, but finally said he would check. He closed the door but did not lock it. Maybe this was her chance thought Tina. She stood and debated with herself and by the time she had decided to make a run for it, the door opened again and she was handed a sandwich and a glass of water. Well at least it was better than nothing.

As she sat down to eat, she began to think of Robert. Where was he and what was was he doing. Was he to eating at the same time, was he even still in town. Stop thinking like that Tina, she said to herself. Of course, he is still in town. He is doing something to get her out of this situation. He had to be, he loves me she thought. Damn, I just wish I knew what was going on; just a tidbit of information would put me at ease. Stop thinking like this you fool, eat this damn sandwich, drink the water and try to get some sleep. You are going to need all the energy you can muster. After choking down the dry bread and thin slice of ham, she downed the water and lay down. Being as tired as she was it did not take her long to drift of to sleep.

At Distefano's everything was good. The red sauce was great and the sausages were fresh. The wines were perfect. The conversation was light and the mood seemed upbeat. After all the other questions, the conversation turned back to Tina, Billy, Mike, Pat and what needed to be done. Robert asked Don why he needed to find a pay phone. The answer left him speechless. "Ok Robert, I know some people down in Columbia. If I am not mistaken, they have connections in Miami. If I'm going to call them, I need to do it from a phone that needs to be clean. No wire taps, no traces, nobody listening." Robert said he understood. "But earlier you said it was going to cost me, just what did you mean?"

"Well if I am not mistaken these people are going to want to get paid for their trouble, I would guess around one hundred thousand."

"One hundred thousand, for what." Robert replied. "I think I can get them to bring a large amount of what they sell out here to show this idiot. He will pay for it but delivery will not be made, if you know what I mean. As I was saying, we win." Robert smiled, this sounded like it just might work. He told Don all he wanted to know was if his friends wanted to be paid in advance or after they go out here. "I really don't know, that is something I will have to discuss with the Columbians when I call."

"What about the assholes who have taken Tina?" Robert asked. "Do you really want to know or can you figure that one out for yourself?" Don asked. After giving this a little thought Robert realized that he knew exactly what would happen to them. He had seen what happened to people that crossed Don, it was not pretty, but it was effective.

As Pat sat at the bar in The Eatery, he was feeling pretty damn good about how things were working out. He had gotten one thousand bucks out of Robert and now he stood to make another twenty-five grand from Billy. He took another drink from the glass in front of him and when he put it down Billy was sitting beside him. "So, you're sure that Robert is not trying to deliver what I ordered from him, he is just trying to get his hands on my cash and run."

"That is what he has always told me he does; besides what does it matter. If he shows up with the shit, he gets the girl and you get what you want." Pat said with his normal grin. "All of that is fine but I want to make sure you understand if anything goes wrong I am holding you personally responsible."

"Look dude, I told you what I know, I helped you get the girl to your house, hell I am in this just as deep as you. All I got to say is I better get my damn money."

"Dude, I am not your dude, not your friend. I'm just paying you for the information and a little assistance. Other than that, you are a nobody to me. Understand?"

"Yeah I understand, just make sure that when this shit is over I get my money." Pat said as indignantly as he could.

Robert glanced at his watch, two in the morning. Things were just as he expected but at least he had heard Don's idea. He was not sure about using the Columbians, but then again he did not know who else to turn to, that was for sure. Now when it came to someone coming from Miami that worried him. He had worked Miami several times and had done very well for himself. He was not sure how well, but he knew it had been worth his time. His could only hope that whoever came up was someone he had never seen before or at least had never worked before. He could only hope.

Don looked at Robert and asked, "What are you thinking about son?" Robert smiled and said, "I was just thinking about what you said earlier, about you ideas to take care of this situation."

"Don't lie to me son, I know that your worried about who my South American friends are and who they send from Miami. Trust me; you have nothing to worry about. I have kept a good eye on you and you never hit any of their people down there. Came close a couple of times but those always fell through. You can thank me later." Don said with a hearty laugh. This information set Robert at ease, well just a bit. However, he had to know more. "When do you think you will be making that phone call?"

"I hope to make it in the morning. Just like you, I want this whole shit pile over as soon as we can. And by the way, we have yet to discuss my fees for helping you solve this little problem." Robert looked at Don, not quite believing what he had just heard but the more he thought about it made sense. Don Vodolchi never did anything without being paid for his services. He got either cash or a promise, and Robert knew in this type of situation it could only be cash. "Ok my ole friend, how much is this going to cost me?"

"We can discuss that when its over, if that is fine with you. Oh, don't forget, when you collect from your favorite asshole, I still get my ten percent." Robert smiled but secretly he just hoped he made some on this whole mess. The least he hoped for was to cover his expenses.

At three in the morning, the three men made their way to the car. The ride back to the Hilton took less than thirty minutes and Robert was grateful, he just wanted Mr. Vodolchi to get some sleep and make the damn phone call. As they stepped in the elevator Don reached into his pocket and handed Bobby a key, you are on the twenty-first floor my friend. Looking at Robert, he smiled and said, "And I am next door to you my son." Robert smiled saying, "It's nice to have a friendly neighbor."

"Don't get to friendly I may not be so nice." Don said with a grin.

After Bobby got off on his floor, Don turned to Robert and said, "Don't worry Robert, have I ever let you down or done you wrong?"

"No sir, never"

"We have had a good run have we not? There is no way I am going to let it be ruined by some low life scum like this Billy. Do you understand what I am saying?" Robert nodded his head. He knew that Mr. Vodolchi was right. He had always been there whenever Robert needed him. Robert thought back on the night they met. He had walked into that restaurant in Little Italy, sat, and waited. He had been told that this was where Mr. Vodolchi ate most nights. He had to meet this man. He had read everything he could find about him. How he had come from nothing, had joined a mob crew in his teens and had been recognized for the work he could get done. He had worked his way up to the rank of Lieutenant and had made his bosses plenty of money. He controlled the docks and therefore all the liquor shipments into New York, he knew which trucks to hit and which ones to let go. He had bought a few bars or after hours clubs as they were known. And the money just poured in.

After a few more years, in a power grab the likes of which New York had never quite seen, Don Vodolchi had grabbed total control of the Lombardo crime family. All Robert wanted to do was meet and talk with this man. He believed he could make him money and all he wanted was to buy protection, protection if and only if he needed. It would also be nice to have a phone number to call in the event the situation deemed it necessary. Moreover, he was prepared to pay. When he walked into the place Robert could hardly believe his eyes, his excitement glowed and all there could see it. After a couple of hours he had finally gone to Mr. Vodolchi's table, introduced himself, and asked if he could have a few minutes of his time. Mr. Vodolchi had agreed, mainly out of curiosity; but when he heard what this kid had to say he was interested. The fact that he had given him fifty thousand dollars certainly did not hurt. The crime boss smiled and said he probably would be interested but it would cost him ten percent of anything he made. Robert was more than happy to agree. And with that, an alliance was made. Now here they were still working together after ten years. Yes, there was respect for one another between them but there was more. Yes, it would be easy to say that they loved each other; each would do almost anything for the other. That was why Don was here and Robert knew it. He was grateful that Don Vodolchi was here in L.A. to help in anyway he could. And yes, what he had just said was very true, Don had never let him down nor had he ever done him wrong. Robert looked at the man and smiled. Yes, it had been a good run and beside the thrill, working with Mr. Vodolchi would probably be what he would miss the most. "Yes sir, I do understand." And with that, the doors opened and the two men stepped out into the hall. They shook hands and Don said, "Get some sleep son; everything will fall in place later today." And with that Don opened the door to his suite and stepped inside

Upon entering his own suite, Robert fixed a drink. He needed to relax before he even thought about sleep.

The phone ringing brought Robert out of deep sleep. Groggily he answered the phone and the voice on the other end was not the voice he had hoped to hear. Billy offered a very cheerful "Good morning." Robert rolled over, looked at the clock, ten o'clock, damn it was too early. "What can I do for you?" Robert asked. "Oh I think you know what I want. I just felt I should tell you that I have the full three-quarters and expect to purchase no less than we have already discussed. When should I expect delivery?"

"I plan on having that answer for you this afternoon, but before we get to that point tell me how Tina is."

"I really don't think you need to worry about that little bitch. However, if you must know, she is fine. Demanding as ever but other than having to get used to being gagged she is alright."

"Let me talk with her."

"Again, I don't think you are in any position to demand anything, is that clear enough."

"Listen Billy, if you want your shipment and if you have any hope of covering your debts you will put her on the damn phone!"

"Ok, settle down and you can speak to your bitch." The next voice Robert heard was music to his ears. "Robert, is that you?' "Yes Tina it is me. Are you alright?"

"Other than being pissed off, I think I am. What is going on?"

"Tina just listen, don't say a word. Everything is going to ok. All that we planned is going to work out. You have to trust and believe me. I can not tell you everything right now but please don't worry it will all work out."

"I do believe you Robert; I just really need to hear one thing from you right now." Robert smiled and said, "I love you." Tina fought back the tears and said, "I love you too." The next thing Robert heard was a scream from Tina and then Billy said, "Now you got what you wanted now make damn sure I get what I want." And with that, the phone went dead.

Robert lay in bed thinking about what had just happened. He was happy that he had spoken with Tina but he was even more pissed at Billy. Who the hell did he think he was? Damn, the only wish he had at this moment was that when Billy got what was coming to him he hoped he was there to see it. Robert could not remember when he had ever hated someone as much as he did Billy. However, he had to admit if it came down between getting Tina back safe and seeing Billy pay his debt in full, he would have to choose Tina. He did love her; he missed her and only wanted to have her back with him safe and sound.

Lying in bed, Robert realized that there was no way he would be able to get back to sleep. With that understanding fresh in his mind, he picked up the phone and ordered some coffee. He took a quick shower and dressed for the day. He wondered if Don was awake but decided it probably was not a good idea to call his suite. No, he needed to relax and be patient. Finally, there was a knock on the door and as he opened the door, he could smell the coffee.

Sitting in the living area, he turned on the television and was happy to see news about something other than the terrorist attacks. It did seem like things were returning to normal. He knew that baseball games had been played last night and soon saw a shot of a bald eagle flying into Yankee Stadium. He had to admit, it was a beautiful picture. With the volume off, he simply sat and watched the picture. In his mind seeing what had taken place in New York last night was better than listening to some pundit describing it.

The phone ringing brought him back to reality. Before he answered the call he glanced at his watch, eleven-thirty, who could this be. Answering the call, he heard the voice he had wished to hear. Don was saying something about coming down. "Hold on Don, I really did not follow that, what did you say."

"Damn man, did I wake you up?"

"No I have been up for a while now, so what were you saying."

"Come downstairs and meet me in the bar."

"I'll be right there." And with that, he hung up the phone and headed out the door.

As he stepped in the bar, he saw Don sitting alone, near the baby grand piano. Walking over to him, he could see that Don was in deep thought. Robert choose to stand by the table and finally Don realized he was there and he motioned for him to take a seat. Sitting in silence was the last thing Robert wished to do. Looking at Don he asked, "Have we found anything out yet?" Don looked up from his coffee and smiled. "Yes, everything is in motion. My call went pretty much as I had hoped and all we need to do is wait for a call from Miami."

"Why is anyone going to call from Miami?"

"They need to know how much shit to bring. We want this to look real, don't we?" Robert had to agree with this logic.

After getting, a refill and a cup for Robert, Don asked, "And what have you been up to this morning?"

"Well I got a call from my favorite asshole." Don smiled and showed interest. Robert continued, "He told me how much cash he had and wanted to know when he could expect delivery. I told him I would be able to call him later this afternoon. He accepted that and other than trying to convince me he was in charge that was it."

"Were you able to discover if Tina is alright?"

"She told me she was fine, other than being pissed off with Billy she is doing ok."

"Wow, you actually talked with her?" Robert laughed and said, "Well I guess Billy really is in charge, wouldn't you agree." Don could not control his laughter. The bartender must have wondered what was so funny. "Robert, I am so happy for you. Now all we need to do is get our ducks in a row and march them right up his ass."

After his second cup of coffee, Robert asked where Bobby was. Don smiled while telling him that he was out taking care of a few things. Do not worry about that son-of-a-bitch he can take care of himself. Robert knew this was a fact. Bobby was one of the most self-assured men he had ever known. One thing that was sure, when it came to Bobby, fear was something he put into other people not something he felt. Robert wanted to know what he was doing but knew better than to ask. No, if Don had wanted him to know or if he felt that he needed to know then he would have told him. Thinking about Bobby, Robert had to smile. He loved the story about how he earned the nickname "the steer." Legend had it that on his first hit, for Don of course, his gun jammed. The hit realized what was going on and took off running as fast as he could. Bobby took off in chase and chased the guy for over a mile. Finally, the guy ran out of gas and slowed way down. Not Bobby, hell no, he keep going as fast as his legs would carry him. Finally, he just ran the guy down. Hit him with so much force the guy was thrown into a brick wall, broke his neck and died on the spot. Ever since then Bobby was called "The Steer." Remembering that story brought a smile to his face. Don saw the smile, was curious but did not ask, he really did not want to hear about Tina.

A few minutes passed with neither man speaking and then Don's cell phone rang. Answer it he smiled and flashed Robert a thumbs up. Robert could not hear what was being said. Don was an expert at speaking a volume that only the person intended to hear what he had to say could hear. No bystander had a chance. When he ended the conversation, Robert did hear him say he would see the person around five. Robert looked at Don and asked, "Miami?" Don shook his head and said they would be flying to an airport just outside the city. "They have a private jet and would be on the ground sometime between three and four and should be at the Hilton no later than five." Robert could feel a sense of relief coming over him but he still had so many questions.

Don picked up on the fact that Robert needed to talk. Looking at

Robert, he asked him to call for a car and they would go eat lunch and hopefully find a quite place so they could talk. Robert smiled and quickly called for a car. Within thirty minutes, Jose had pulled up outside and the two men made their way outside. Robert got in the car as Don was talking with Jose. After a few minutes, Don joined Robert in the back seat and said, "Got everything taken care, just sit back and relax."

To the great surprise to Robert, Jose had stopped at a sandwich shop. Jose got out of the car and disappeared inside the joint. Don and Robert remained in the car but neither said a word. After several minutes Jose was back behind the wheel and they were on the way again. After about fifteen minutes, the car pulled into the parking lot of Dodger Stadium. Robert and Don got out of the car and Jose handed Don the bag from the sandwich shop. Following Don, Robert found himself entering the stadium after Don spoke with a man at the gate. Soon they were sitting on the third base side enjoying the meatball sandwiches. Finally, Don turned to Robert and began, "This is what I have set up, the guy from Miami, Jorge, is bringing enough kilos to give Billy a heart attack. He is also going to have a couple of friends tagging along. Between the three of them there will be enough heat to raise the outside temperature at least twenty degrees. Since you set this damn thing up you will be the point man. You do all the talking with Billy. The main thing is we need the exchange to be somewhere closed in. That way, no witnesses. Bobby tells me that son-of-a-bitch took your gun when he took the girl. He is going to have a piece for you, don't want to go into this with no protection. Once you got the cash and the girl I would suggest you twos get the hell out of there. Jorge, his two friends, and Bobby are going to have some fun, and you better believe it is going to get real wet." Robert nodded his head in understanding. He knew that real wet meant it was going to be bloody. He guessed that the shooters planned to inflict more than a little pain before they finished the job. "Mr. Vodolchi, I will never be able to make this right by you. All I can say is thank you and to me that is not enough."

"Ok, Ok, enough of all that sentimental crap, Listen you big shit, I aint doing this so much for you, it's for the girl. I figure any girl that agrees to marry you is worth saving. Besides, nobody, I mean nobody fucks with anyone that works for me. That fucker, Billy, gots this coming." Robert smiled, he knew Don was a little pissed but he surely did know how to take care of business.

They left the stadium around one o'clock and made their way back to the Hilton. It had been agreed on to contact Billy around two and try to get the exchange set up sometime tonight. Just as Robert and Don were getting out of the car Don's cell rang. He answered it and immediately became pissed. Robert could not quite hear what was being discussed; it was obvious that there was a problem. Then he heard Don say, "Get the damn thing fixed, find another, and get your ass out here." Slamming the flip phone closed Don looked at Robert and said, "My suite, now, I need a drink!" In Don's suite, drinks were made and made strong. Don turned and said, "There is a problem in Houston."

"Houston, what the hell is going on in Texas and what the hell does it have to do with us in L.A.?" asked Robert. "There seems to be a problem with the jet from Miami. They had to put down in Houston, and are hoping to get it fixed. I told them to either fix the damn thing or get another. Either way they will give me a call and let us know what's going on but I don't think they will make it out here 'till tomorrow. Sorry kid." Robert downed his drink in one long swallow.

After pouring himself another drink Robert slumped in the closest chair. With everything going on, he had allowed himself to think about being with Tina tonight and it now appeared that that was now out of the question. His thoughts were totally consumed by her. He could not get the sound of desperation in her voice out of his mind, from when they had spoken on the phone earlier. He knew he could not dwell on these thoughts but it was hard to shake them.

Don had gone to the bedroom and now was stepping out as he headed back to the bar. Looking at Robert, he could see the pain on his face and knew exactly what he had been thinking about. "Robert, you gotta stop kicking yourself in the ass over all of this. There was no way that you could of have seen any of this coming. I just got of the phone with Houston. They think they will be out here by early in the morning."

"Fine, I'll call Billy and get the exchange set up first thing tomorrow."

"No, I think we better wait on that call until we know exactly when they will be here. No sense in jumping the gun. Have another drink and when Bobby gets back we will head out for dinner."

After his third drink, Robert was starting to relax. He knew everything was going to work out he just needed to be patient. Start looking at this just like any other job, he thought. You have always been able to wait on things to come together and always have it right. Tina is a strong girl, she will make it through this and besides, Billy may be dumb but he is not stupid. He is not going to cause her any harm other than holding her hostage. He knows better than to mess with anyone's fiancée, or at least he better. With the understanding of what he needed to do and how he needed to be thinking Robert was starting to feel that everything would work out. He went to the bar and poured another drink.

Just as Robert sat back down there was a knock on the door. Don got up and opened the door, allowing Bobby to come in. He went straight to the bar and fixed a drink. Walking towards a chair, he dropped a 9mm in Robert's lap. "Be careful with that, it's loaded." Robert smiled; it was nice to have a piece again. Don got up and the two of them went to the bedroom. Robert hollered at Don and told him he was going next door to his suite and when they finished up to come on over, he would leave the door unlocked. Stepping into his own suite, he headed straight for the shower.

After getting dressed, Robert stepped out of the bedroom to find Bobby and Don sitting in the living area. The two of them were laughing and enjoying a drink. Don looked up and gave Robert a whistle saying, "Now that is what I call a suit!" Robert smiled and said, "You better like it, you bought it for me last fall."

"Of course, I remember. That was right after you showed up with two hundred thousand dollars, my cut out of the biggest hit you ever made. Two million from some Hollywood actor type if I remember."

THE FINAL SCORE

"Your memory never has let you down Mr. Vodolchi." Robert said with a smile. Both men got a chuckle out of what was being said and the memory of the transaction they were remembering. "Fix a drink and grab a seat, we have a few things to talk about and then were going to get some dinner." Don told him.

After fixing the drink, Robert took a seat and waited. Don finally began talking, "Bobby discovered that his first thought was correct. The girl is at the house that is being watched by the two black guys. The best thing is it is just the two of them, at least on the outside. Your friend Billy seems to keeping up appearances as he left this morning and has been at The Eatery all day. I guess the asshole is just waiting on your call."

"Well I guess I will just make him happy and drop the call on him right now."

"No you don't. I already told you we make that call only when we know for sure that the boys from Miami are here."

"When they are here, I thought you said when we knew what time they would be here."

"Yeah that is what I said but I talked with them about thirty minutes ago and their jet will be ready in the morning and they will be out here sometime after that. Since we will not know when they're leaving, we will just wait until they call once they have landed. That way there will be no fuck up. All of this should be over by this time tomorrow." At least Robert now knew that everything was on track and if no more problems popped up it would all be over. "Wait a minute, Bobby, how do you know for sure she is at the house?"

"When I drove by there earlier today I saw a girl looking out a window on the side of the house. She had shoulder length dark hair. Description sound right?"

"Yeah that sounds right," replied Robert. With that, Don announced it was time to eat.

The car stopped in front of Distefano. Robert looked up and smiled. This was so much like Don. Show him a good Italian restaurant and he was like a dog with a bone. There was no way he would let it go. Granted, the food was good and the service was nice but damn, a big steak would go down real good about now, Robert thought. Oh well, at least it would be another good meal and probably a good time. Stepping inside the first thing Robert noticed was no one else was there. Obviously, Don had made a phone call. Sure enough, a well-dressed man, probably the owner, called out, "Mr. Vodolchi, it is so nice to see you again!"

"Mr. Distefano, thank you so much for inviting me and my friends back for a good meal, good vino, and a quiet night. Your hospitality will be rewarded and I will never forget you or your place." And, with that, the three men were shown to a table in the middle of the room. After sitting down Robert watched Mr. Distefano lock the door and put up the closed sign. Damn, Don Vodolchi really knew how to plan a night out in a strange town, Robert thought with a smile.

The meatballs, pasta, red sauce, and garlic bread just kept coming. Of course, the wine never stopped being poured. It was easy to tell that the two waiters knew that whoever they were taking care were important. The respect they showed was genuine and the service was excellent. So excellent that Robert had to tell them not to change the ashtray just because he had just flicked the ashes off his cigarette. Somewhere after the second course and before the fourth course the conversation turned to the planned events of tomorrow.

Don looked at Robert and said, "You need to tell Billy that you will have his shipment by three in the afternoon. Once the exact place is set up, let's hope it is his house; make sure to get a time. You will then show up thirty minutes early. The good guys will show up a few minutes later. Once Bobby, I, and the guys from Miami are in get the girl out of there. Make sure to take the cash with you. Speaking of cash, you will need to have the one hundred grand for Jorge before any of this goes down. You see, the Columbians expect payment up front, no exceptions. You can make sure of that can't you?" Robert said he could and reminded Don about the conversation they had already had pertaining to cash. Don smiled, remembering and said, "Make sure you arrange a trip to the safe with the hotel staff, we don't need any money problems tomorrow." And then, "Bobby, are all the guns clean, you know, no serial numbers."

"Cut me a brake Don, you know I don't make mistakes like that. Even the one I gave Robert is clean. Don't worry; there will be no problems on my end."

"Ok, everything seems to be in place, except the shit, but it is on its way, let's all relax and enjoy the rest of the evening." With that, the fifth course arrived and all continued to eat and drink.

Upon getting back to the Hilton, Robert went to the front desk to inquire about getting into the safe. He was told that he would be given access at any time after seven in the morning. As he walked to the elevator, Pat stepped out of the restrooms. He walked up to Robert and asked if he could come up to his room, there were a few things that needed to be talked about. Robert said that would be fine and the two headed to the elevator.

As the doors opened on Robert's floor Bobby was standing there waiting. He looked at both men, and said good evening and step into the elevator. Robert glanced over his shoulder as he walked down the hall and took note of the fact that Bobby had gotten off the elevator. Upon getting to his suite, he opened the door and allowed Pat to go in ahead of him. Stepping inside Robert closed the door, making sure it did not latch. As he stepped out of the hall and into the living area he saw Pat at the bar fixing two cocktails. He turned around and offered a glass to Robert who took it and set in on the table beside his chair. Pat sat on the couch and looking at Robert he said, "Listen bro, I know you're pissed at me but hey you gotta understand that money is money."

"I understand that you will do just about anything for cash but kidnapping is even low for you, is it not."

"Slow down big guy, taking the girl was all Billy's idea, we came by here to see you, you know to try to put a little pressure on you and found out you were not here. The girl had no idea where you were and Billy freaked out. That was when he grabbed her; put a gun in her back and the three of us just walked out of here."

"Ok let's say I believe you and all your bullshit, what are you doing here and what do you have to say to me."

"Listen, all I was trying to do was sell some information to Billy; you know just trying to pick up some quick cash. All I told him was to be careful because sometimes your mule gets busted. Once I told him that he went ballistic and I already told you what happened next. But the reason I am here tonight is to warn you."

"Warn me?"

"Yeah, the exchange is suppose to take place at Billy's and if things go the way he's got it planned in his head both you and the girl are going to die."

"And where are you going to be while we're getting dead?"

"Man I am out of here, got my cash and plane ticket home in my pocket and I am out of here. Just be careful my friend, hope everything works out for both you and the girl." With that, Pat stood up and headed for the door. As he opened the door, the last thing he saw was a fist.

Robert spilled his drink when he jumped at what he had just seen. Bobby was stepping over Pat who was knocked out cold, and forcing the door closed, he said, "Sounds like things just might get interesting tomorrow." Robert had to agree, "When do you think we should tell Don?" Bobby smiled and said, "He already was expecting something like this, which is why he wants everything to roll before the time you set up." Robert realized that this was not going to go down the way he wanted, all nice and quite. No, the shit was going to be deep and he was standing right in the middle of the pile.

Robert told Bobby he needed to get some sleep and headed to the bedroom. Bobby said that was fine, he would take care of the sleeping beauty. Not too long after Robert went to bed Pat began to come around. As he opened his eyes, he saw Bobby. Sitting up he asked, "Who the hell are you?"

"I'm your worst nightmare, that's who I am." With that, Bobby kicked Pat square in the face, knocking him back out. This patterned repeated itself several times throughout the night. Every time Pat regained consciousness Bobby made sure he went back to sleep. Damn Bobby thought, I could get use to having fun like this.

Robert awoke as the sun was shinning into the bedroom window. He looked at the clock on the nightstand and saw that it was only seven-thirty. After taking a quick shower, he dressed and headed out to the living area. As he stepped through the door, the first thing he saw was Pat. He looked like he had been put through a blender. His eyes were swollen shut, his lips were the size of doughnuts, there was blood coming from his ears, damn he looked bad. It took Robert a few minutes before he was sure Pat was breathing, he was, damn it. Bobby looked up and smiled. "Did you get some rest?" he asked. Robert nodded as he reached for the phone to call room service for some coffee. Looking back at Pat he said, "Looks like you were busy." Bobby laughed saying, "Yeah, the asshole just would not stay asleep, so I had to help him just a bit." This brought a loud laugh from Robert. He had to be honest with himself, Pat was a decent person, for an asshole, but he did deserve the butt kicking he obviously took. He could only wonder when Bobby would finish the job. The more he thought about it realized he really did not care. If Pat was killed for involvement in all of this Robert figured he deserved what he got even though he did come here last night in hopes of warning him about what was being planned for his arrival. Looking at Bobby again he asked, "What are you planning on doing with what is left of Pat?"

"What would you like to have happen to him?"

"Hell I really don't know. He is the one person who is responsible for all this shit but he did come here to warn me."

THE FINAL SCORE

"Well then, let's just say that he will meet his maker with a clean conscious." And with that, the conversation about Pat was over.

At eight o'clock, there was a knock on the door. Robert got up expecting his coffee was here, but when he opened the door, Don stepped in. When he saw Pat, all he could do was smile. Looking at Bobby he asked, "Had a little fun last night did we?" Bobby looked up and smiled. After some small talk between the three men, another knock on the door stopped the talking. Robert went to the door and was happy to see the coffee was here. Pouring cups for everyone, he returned to the living area and sat down opposite of Don. All three men drank their coffee and just kept looking at Pat. He was beginning to come around and Don told Bobby it was probably time to get him out of here. Bobby agreed and when Pat had regained consciousness Bobby helped him to his feet and walked him out of the suite. Robert understood that he would not see Pat again.

A few minutes after Bobby and the bloody mess had made their way out of the suite Don's cell phone rang. Answering the phone Don headed towards the bedroom. Robert hoped that the call was from the guys from Miami. He was ready for all of this to be over. What he really wanted was to have Tina back by his side.

About fifteen minutes later Don came out of the bedroom. Looking at Robert he said, "Time to pay the piper my friend. The boys are here; at least they will be here within the hour. Go ahead and call your boy. Set the exchange up for; let's try for noon. If that isn't good then shoot for two. Either way that gives us enough time to arrive early. Like I said last night, we want to at least try to catch them off guard. I do not think we are dealing with any professionals here, so it won't take much to gain the advantage. Anyway, go ahead and make that call and we will talk after you find out what time." Robert shook his head and went into the bedroom to call Billy.

The phone was answered on the second ring. "Billy, Robert, everything is almost ready. All I need to know is where and what time."

"Oh man that sounds great. Why don't we get together this afternoon, would one or two be better for you?"

"Well it depends on where."

"How about my house, that way I don't have to go anywhere or do anything but wait."

"Your place at two sounds fine with me, let's make it two. Now please put Tina on the phone."

"Well I see you still have not learned. One of these days someone is just going to have to teach you that you can't boss people around."

"Slow down there cowboy, if you would just think back a couple of minutes you would remember I said please."

"Ok, you're right about that, but it was the way you said it. So if you think you can say it again and this time with no attitude I just might allow you to speak to the bitch!" Taking a deep breath Robert tried again, "Billy, may I please speak to Tina?"

"Now was that so damn difficult? Hang on and I'll get her." After several minutes, Robert heard Tina saying hello.

"Hey sweetie, how are you?"

"I am alright I just want to get the hell out of here!"

"I understand, now listen I have some things to tell you but before I do is anyone else around?"

"Yeah but not too close if you catch my drift."

"Yeah I got it, now listen and listen carefully. We have the exchange set up for two; the only thing is I will be there about thirty minutes early. Not too long after that, all hell is going to brake out. You and I will be getting the hell out of there, hopefully before things get bad but either way we will be on our way."

"How is all this supposed to happen?"

"Listen Tina, this is one of those things that you're just going to have to trust me and react when I tell you to. Do you understand?"

"Well I think you two have talked enough." It was Billy. Robert hoped that he had not heard anything or if he did, he did not understand. It was a chance he would have to take. "Ok Billy, I'll see you at two."

"Yeah and don't be late." And with that, the phone went dead.

Walking back out to be with Don, Robert sat down and said, "It is on for two."

"Good. Is it going to be at his house?"

"Yeah that is where he wants it. Said something about not wanting to have to go anywhere or something like that." Don chuckled hearing this. He seemed to take pleasure that the whole thing would be going down there and not somewhere else. This caused several questions to run through Roberts' mind but he decided he would rather not know the answers.

Don had ordered more coffee and was enjoying a cup when his phone rang. Upon answering the call it did not take Robert long to realize that it was Bobby. As the conversation continued, he came to the understanding that Pat was dead. Don also took a minute to inform Bobby that the exchange would be taking place at two and it would be at Billy's house. Upon ending the conversation, Don turned to Robert and said, "Bobby has taken care of the first problem and it is easy for me to say that that is one problem that we will not have to worry about anymore. He is also pleased to know the time and said he would meet us there."

"So it sounds like everything is coming together."

"Listen my friend, I told you I would make sure it all happened and it will. You need to relax and trust me. Now when the boys from Miami get here they are going to give you a case that will have all the shit. At that time, you will give them the money. I doubt they will count it, but if you don't want to spend the rest of your life looking over your shoulder you had better make sure it is exactly one hundred grand. When we get to the house, everything will go on you. In other words, you will be the point man. It is going to be up to you how you handle things. The two most important things for you to remember are you need to get both the cash and the girl away from the asshole. Can you do it?" Robert gave this some thought before responding. "I think I can pull it off, I just don't want to do anything that might fuck this whole thing up."

"If I did not think you could handle it I would not put you in that position. All you need to do is remain cool. And don't forget, the tuff shit is going to be on the rest of us. I know you got the gun Bobby gave you but I don't want to see it."

"But what if I don't have a choice?"

"Well, all I can say is use your own judgment, but don't forget the money and the girl."

"Those are two things I will not forget about." Don could not hold back his smile. He did love this man and would be heartbroken if anything happened to either him or the girl. No matter what he had to do to make sure that did not happen.

When that conversation had ended Don told Robert he needed to go down and get the cash out of the safe. Robert agreed and made his way down to the front desk. As he stepped up to the desk a young man said, "Good morning Mr. McGuire, how can I help you this morning?" Robert smiled and said, "I need to get something out of the safe."

"Yes Sir, if you will just follow me." Robert followed the young man down a short hall and into a small room that had multiple safe deposit boxes built into the wall. The young man took a couple of keys out of his coat pocket and looking at a clipboard said, "Here it is." And with that, he unlocked one of the boxes and then stepped back. Robert looked at him as if to say, I would like some privacy and the young man seemed to understand. With that, he opened the door and said, "I will wait out here and when you are finished just close your box and I'll replace it and lock it back up." Robert smiled and watched the young man step out of the room. With the box opened, Robert began removing bundles of cash out of it and counting the strapped bundles twice to make sure it was one hundred grand. Putting the cash inside his coat pockets he closed the box. He decided to place the box in its slot and then he opened the door. The young man re-entered the room, locked the box and the two men again stepped out of the room. As they made their way back towards the lobby Robert turned and asked, "Could you assist me in finding a large envelope?" The young man smiled and asked Robert to accompany him back to the front desk, as he was sure he could find something to his liking. At the front desk, Robert was handed a manila envelope that was at least ten inches by twelve inches. Robert thought this would be fine and thanked the young man and headed to the elevator.

THE FINAL SCORE

Stepping back into his suite Robert could not wait to get the cash into the envelope. Stepping into the living area, he stopped at the coffee table, and pulled the cash out of his coat and began to carefully place the bundles inside and made sure it would close. It took a little effort but he was finally able to get the silver clasp to close and with that, the money thing was taken care of. The whole time Robert was messing with the envelope he could sense Don's eyes riveted on him and what he was doing. Finally, Don said, "Damn son, maybe you should go fix yourself a drink and celebrate accomplishing that small little feat." Both Robert and Don got a chuckle out of this. Robert instead poured himself what turned out to be the last cup of coffee. Setting the carafe back on the table he asked Don if he would like some more coffee and Don simply shook his head to indicate the negative.

The two men sat in the relative quite, the only noise was the television set with the volume down low. Each man was deep in his own, private thoughts. It was easy to see that those thoughts were primarily consumed with what they faced but neither thought it to be important to discuss anything. What had needed to be talked about had already been discussed, now they waited. Much like an expectant father waiting on his first-born. As they sat, the one thing in common was the desire for the boys from Miami to show up. At least when that happened they would know that their plan would be put into motion. Until that had occurred, the only thing they could do was to sit, think, and watch the clock.

At twelve-fifteen, a knock was heard at the door. Robert looked at Don who was checking the time. He was the first to move. He stood up and motioned for Robert to remain seated. He made his way to the door and upon opening it, three men were waiting in the hall. He took a step back and allowed the men to come in, in silent single file. The first man looked at Don and smiled. He was carrying a rather large suitcase and when he placed it on the floor, he turned to Don and with arms outstretched, and he took a step toward him. Don responded in kind and when the two men met, they hugged and kissed each other on the cheeks. The other two men stood back and allowed these two to greet one another. After the hug, the first man introduced the others. The first was Wayne and the second was Henry. Wayne appeared at ease meeting Don and did not hesitate to attempt to start a conversation. Don just looked at him and moved on to meet the second man, Henry. Don then turned and led the way to the living room where he introduced Robert to Jorge Columbo, Wayne, and Henry. Robert took note that Jorge was middle aged while Wayne was probably a few years younger but Henry appeared to be the oldest. Wayne continued to talk even though no one was paying a bit of attention to him. He began to tell a story, with himself as the main character, something about having a Bell Jet Helicopter, but still no one was listening. This did not appear to have any effect on Wayne; he just kept talking. Finally, Don looked at him and said, "Man can you shut the fuck up!" Wayne gave Don a look that resembled a child being corrected by a parent and it was apparent that Don could care less. Robert, having known Don for the past ten years, knew that anyone who talked to himself would suffer the consequences of doing so in front of Don. Watching this brought a smile to Robert's face and in a strange sense, he was grateful for the smile.

Don and Jorge had been discussing something that Robert had no clue as Wayne had been drowning them out. Don turned to Robert and asked, "Robert where is the envelope?" With that, Robert got up, went to the bedroom, and returned with what had been asked for. Jorge stood up and stuck out his hand in a way that made it obvious to Robert that he were the one expecting the payment. Handing the envelope to Jorge, Robert sat down and watched. Just as Don had said, the money was not counted. Instead, Jorge simply opened it up; upon peering inside, he closed the clasp, and laid the envelope down on the coffee table. Robert was impressed by the nonchalance of how Jorge handled the payment. He had to admit, to someone in his line of work, seeing another handle a large amount of money with what appeared to be no true regard was refreshing. This act gave rise to another smile.

It did not take long for the conversation between Don and Jorge to turn to the upcoming events of the afternoon. Don did a good job of explaining what he would like to see happen. Jorge turned to his two men and told them to go down to the lobby and wait for the rest of us. After they were gone, Jorge turned to Don and said, "Mr. Vodolchi, I know you only by reputation and I must admit that that reputation is one of honor. It is at this time that I must tell you what I need." Don leaned forward saying; "I am open to most suggestions but do you wish to talk with me about anything you value in front of Robert."

"What I have to say involves him so I will speak openly. The two idiots I have with me are here for a reason. First, it must be understood, that they will not be coming back to Miami with me. And as I understand the situation that we have out here there are steps that I feel that need to be taken to assure that no one will ask too many questions." Don interrupted asking, "And what are you asking of me?"

"Mr. Vodolchi, the men with me are not like you and I, let us say they are more like your friend here, Robert." Don Vodolchi knew exactly what that meant. What was being told to him was that neither of these men was made, in other words, neither were full members of the crime family in Miami. "I understand what you are saying, what is the problem and how may I help?" The problem is these men know some things that they should not and my boss fears that the way these two drink and talk, he worries that they will spill their guts in a moment of lust or drunkenness. With that being understood my boss wishes for these two to be left out here in a manner that they will never speak again."

"I know your boss and he too has a reputation that is one of honor. If it is his desire to have this happen then who am I to question or deny. It shall happen." Jorge smiled and continued, "This will also help the situation out here. As I see it, after the wet stuff is done I will leave a busted kilo on a table so that it will appear to be nothing more than a drug deal gone bad. I do believe that this will allow all others to slip away with little to no attention." Don smiled at Jorge and again said that this would not be a problem. Jorge turned to Robert and said, "I understand form my boss that this fucked up mess is your doing, is that correct?"

"Yes it is my deal that has gone bad," said Robert. Jorge smiled and continued, "I like a man that takes responsibility for his own actions, and in doing so you have saved yourself some money." Robert looked at Jorge and it was obvious to all in the room that he did not quite understand what he was being told. Jorge smiled and asked, "The envelope you gave me earlier is that the one hundred grand that you were told this would cost?"

"Yes and I counted it twice to make sure it is the correct amount." Upon hearing this confession from Robert, Jorge could not help but laugh. Collecting himself he said, "Well I am glad you are careful and I appreciate your diligence, now I need you to take fifty grand out of the envelope. For you see, your situation has given my boss the opportunity to take care of a problem that he wishes to and he is very pleased that it can be done somewhere instead of his fair city. Therefore the charge for our help will be half of what you were told." Robert smiled and did not hesitate to express his gratitude and appreciation. This was done with extreme respect and in seeing this Jorge turned to Don and asked, "Mr. Vodolchi may I inquire as to why this man, who is openly respectful to the two of us, why is not a made man?" Don smiled and leaned forward and said, "I understand your question but the answer is very painful to me. You see, this man has become one that I trust in all matters, I know he would gladly give his life to protect mine. He would do anything I ask; as he has during the entire time we have known one another. I am glad to see you recognize his qualities that I have grown to love. The problem is, and this pains me to no end, he is not Italian. No, this big son-of-a-bitch is Irish." The laughter that came from the man from Miami was so loud Robert knew it could be heard at the far end of the hall.

Don called the car service and requested a stretch limo as there would be five making the trip to Billy's house. All three men took the time to have a drink and the conversation soon turned to the events in New York back on the eleventh. Don showed the pain he felt when he said. "Those bastards don't know who they fucked with. I am tempted to try to contact the President and offer mine and my men's talents to help track that Osama guy down and put his head on a stick. I mean who the hell does he think he is, to send some of his flunkies to my house and do that kind of damage." Jorge was quick to add, "That is exactly how I feel about all of this. I mean the government would stop at nothing to put me out of business and probably would celebrate the fact that they have my ass locked away for what would be the rest of my life. Understanding that the government is anything but my friend, but I love this country. My father came here from Sicily and created a life for himself and his family. He loved this country almost as much as his homeland and when push came to shove he would have done just about anything for it." Robert and Don both shook their heads in understanding. They knew that the words Jorge Colombo had said were true and came from his heart. Robert, being the only one who had not addressed the event felt out of place, so leaning forward, he said, "I watched the events of last Tuesday as they unfolded on the television. I must be honest; it took everything I had to fight back the tears as those buildings came down. Now, while I am not connected as the two of you are, I would also do anything the government asked of me to assure that justice would be done." Don smiling at Robert said, "Son with your unique talents I bet the government could use you to find that son-of-a-bitch." Robert smiled and then said, "What talents are you speaking of Don?" Laughingly Don looked at Jorge and said, "This man could sell ice cubes to Eskimos if he thought he could make buck." All three men laughed at hearing this. Jorge turned to Robert and asked, "Could you explain to me just what you do and how you do it?" Robert smiled and began, "I try to find people that are in the need to make a large amount of cash in a short period of time. After spending some time with them and gaining their trust, I simply let them know that I might be able to help them out of their problems. If they are interested, and most are, I explain that I know someone who can sell them enough pure cocaine that they can sell and normally raise at least twice what they owe."

"That is all there is to it?" asked Jorge. "Well almost, I make it clear that the drugs and the money will never be in the same place, for safety reasons. Therefore, I get the cash and they go to meet the drugs. And of course since there never were any drugs, no drugs show up."

"And no one has ever tried to hunt you down to get their money back?"

"Not if I have done my job right. You see, when they contact me, I tell then that the courier was busted and due to that fact, we both lost. I don't have their money; I was only the middle man." Jorge broke into loud laughter. Robert could see that he enjoyed hearing what he had been told. Finally, Jorge asked, "What about the law, how do you stay away from them?" Robert smiled and simply said, "Ever heard of anyone going to the cops to complain about being ripped off in a drug deal?" Again, Jorge threw his head back and roared his approval. All three men got a laugh out of this. Robert wondered if Don was laughing with Jorge or at him. Robert knew that Don had a habit of finding humor at someone else's expense. Who was he to find fault in the man that came personally to help as opposed to sending some of his men? Robert knew that he would always be in Don Volodchi's debt, but that was something he could live with. Besides, the only thing that he was concerned about now was putting an end to all this madness and having Tina back at his side.

Before they left, the three men went over how this whole thing was going to go down. Jorge was pleased to hear that Robert and the drugs would go in first. He liked the idea that he and Don would follow Wayne and Henry, as this would make it easier to kill them. Robert asked Don where Bobby was and was told he should be in the house by now. "In the house, how?"

"You don't tell me all of your little secrets so please don't ask me to tell to you all of mine" Don said with a smile. And with that, he announced it was time to be on their way.

As the three men entered the lobby, they wasted no time in spotting Wayne and Henry. Of course, it was not difficult; all they had to do was listen for Wayne's loud mouth. When Jorge's two idiots saw him, they stopped talking and stood waiting instructions. The five men stepped outside just as the limo was pulling up. Wayne, acting on what Jorge told him opened the door and allowed both Don and Jorge in followed by Henry. Robert told Wayne to go ahead as he would be the first out.

Once the car had left the Hilton Mr. Vodolchi began to tell Wayne and Henry how this thing was going to go down. He made sure that they understood that they were to go in before him and Jorge. Wayne began asking all sort of questions like the lay-out of the house, where people were going to be, and who all had guns. Don looked at Jorge as if to say what a fuck up. Jorge snapped his fingers to get Wayne's attention and told him, "This really is not that difficult, all you need to know is that when we go in everybody with the exception of Robert and the girl are going to wish they had never seen any of us. Does that make it clear enough asshole?" Wayne again lowered his head like the child being fussed at by a parent. He said, "I understand, everything is clear." Jorge gave him a slight grin but choose not to say anything. Don leaned forward and said, "Ok, now that we are all on the same page, I want to let you guys know that I have a man already in the house. It is my hope that he managed to get in without being noticed, and he is just lying low and waiting on us. Now Robert, it is up to you to make sure that all the others are in the room with you, Billy, and the drugs. I am going to leave this up to you as to how you are going to accomplish this little feat, but I have all the faith that you can pull this off. If the cash is not in an envelope or case simply, take the shit out of the briefcase you have and put it in there. Make sure that Tina is close to you. That way when the shooting breaks out you can protect her, at least get her on the floor. Do you understand?" Robert turned and looked directly at Don and nodded his head to indicate that he did in fact understand. Don raised his hand and spoke directly to Robert, "Son, I need to hear you say that you understand."

"I understand Mr. Vodolchi." Robert said as he locked his eyes on Don's. Don returned the look and gave his young friend a smile.

Robert looked at his watch, twelve twenty-five, plenty of time he thought. The men rode in silence and Robert sat and looked out the window. He was thinking of Tina. How he hoped she was all right, would she get through this with out being harmed, would she hold all this against him or could she look past it all and still want to have a life with him. God how he wished he knew the answers to these questions. All he wanted was to be on the beach in Aruba with her. They would do so many things ranging from scuba diving, parasailing, to trying their luck in one of the casinos on the island. They would leave all their cloths here in L.A. and get completely new wardrobes on the island. They would stay out all night; sleep all day not a worry in the world. Yeah he would have to spend an hour or two setting things up at the bank but other than that, it would just be fun. Hell, he might even buy them each a set of golf clubs so they could relax on the course. If she did not know how to play, he would get her lessons. He did not care what they did; he just wanted to be with her. And be with her I will, he thought. Closing his eyes Robert began to run through the upcoming events. He knew he needed to keep his mind clear; otherwise, he might make a mistake. A mistake, he knew, would be disastrous. If anything went wrong, everyone involved could be killed. He had to make sure that did not happen. Where is Bobby he thought? Has he taken a chance to try to find Tina? If not, where is he hiding? Damn, so many questions and no answers. He knew the answers would come soon enough; he just had to be patient. Damn how he hated having to remind himself to be patient. Granted this was going to end very different from any job he had ever pulled off, but it was really the same.

Now instead of the drugs being miles away, waiting to be picked up, they would be right there. There, with the mark, the money, the extra muscle, the drugs all in one place. He knew that when the Miami boys came in all hell was going to break loose. He could only hope that Tina, Don, Bobby and himself made it out in one piece. He had no allegiance to Jorge, but if he made it out ok that would be fine too. He knew that Wayne and Henry would be dead. He looked at both men and wondered if they had any idea what was in store for them. He allowed himself a moment to wonder just what they knew and if they even were aware of it. The thought of the two men sitting in front of him would be dead in a little while made a cold chill run down his spine. However, if their death brought him together with Tina and saved him fifty thousand dollars at the same time, then so be it. After all, they meant absolutely nothing to him. All of these thoughts brought a slight smile to his face. He was beginning to feel comfortable with all of his thoughts and with what was about to happen. Checking his watch again, it was one; the whole thing would begin in less than thirty minutes. He needed to clear his mind and get ready.

As the car slowed to a stop, one could have cut the tension in the car with a knife. Robert took a deep breath and tried to swallow, his mouth was too dry. After a few moments, Robert reached for the door but Don began to speak so he stopped. "Don't worry Robert, Bobby is inside and we got your butt covered. Just do everything as we have already talked about and you will be fine." Robert looked at Don and tried his best to give him a smile. Opening the door Robert stepped out of the car and for the first time looked around. He had to be honest; the view from up here was nice. Looking to the west, he could see all of L.A. spread out in front of him. Damn, it was majestic. As the beauty of the city was being realized he suddenly thought about what he had to do. With that in mind, he began to walk towards the front door.

Stepping up to the door Robert reached for the doorbell, but the door opened even before he had rung the bell. The door was only open a few inches so Robert began to push it further. The door had moved about six inches when it stopped. A few moments later, he heard Billy asking who it was. "It's Robert who else were you expecting."

"Ok, come on in and no funny business you understand." Robert pushed the door completely open and stepped inside. Billy looked like he had not slept over the last few days. It took every bit of self-control for Robert not to chuckle at the sight that stood in front of him. The two men just stared at one another; neither really knew what to say. Finally, Billy asked, "What's in the briefcase?" Robert replied, "It's what you have been waiting for. I told you I would get it for you and here it is." Billy started to move towards the living room and Robert pushed the door closed making sure it did not latch. Realizing his good luck, helped him to relax, with the door not latched the others would be able to get in without making a bit of noise.

Stepping into the living room, Robert was met with the sight of Tina, being held by one of the black men who had a gun to her head. At seeing him, she called out his name and the black man pulled her arm up tighter up her back. The scream that escaped her lips was deafening. Robert looked at Billy and said, "Hey man, have him back off of her, I got your shit, there is no reason for anybody to get hurt"

"There you go again, always trying to call the shots. One of these days your going to learn that you aint shit. You can't tell anyone what to do, let alone when to do it."

"You're right man; I just don't care to see her hurt. I got your shit right here why not let her go." Billy turned to the person who was holding Tina and nodded his head in Roberts's direction. With that being done, Tina was released and she ran to Robert. They hugged and kissed each other. Both were happy but they both knew that this ordeal was far from over. While they were hugging Robert was able to whisper in her ear saying, "I am not alone. Help is near by, just be ready to react." Tina looked up at him, smiled, and nodded to indicate that she understood. Robert could only hope that she did in fact understand but he knew better. She has never been in a situation like this, and he knew that for a fact there was no way she could be even remotely prepared for what was going to go down over the next half hour. But at least he had been able to give her a heads up, all he could do now was whatever it took protect her.

Billy was quick to make a smartass remark, something about the lovebirds and then told Robert that it was time to get down to business. Robert acknowledged what Billy had said and moved towards a large table in the middle of the room. Placing the briefcase on the table he turned to Billy and asked, "Where is the money?" Billy turned and walked down the hall saying he would be right back. Just like this asshole, Robert thought, always running his mouth and did not even have the cash with him. Stay calm he thought, the others are just a few minutes away.

Billy returned carrying a large red duffle bag. Placing it on the table he said, "I guess you are going to count it."

"You bet your ass I am going to count it. With some of the events that you have put into play over the past few days your trust factor is all but used up."

"Oh damn, I am so sorry to hear that. Like I really give a shit about my trust factor when it comes to you. All you are is a damn drug dealer. Hell, look at me, I own my restaurant, this house, a nice ride and you are a damn drug dealer just one-step away from a prison cell for the rest of your life. You probably know that I am hooked up with the law and if I wanted to, you would be locked up now with just one little phone call." Robert did not like the way Billy was talking. He could not determine if this asshole was just making threats or if this whole thing was a set up. There was nothing he could do about it now. At least Don was in the car and if something like that was going to come down, he could get away. "Yeah you could make that call and fuck me over real good, but then you would not be able to get even with the IRS and JD." Billy gave Robert a little smile knowing the words just spoken were very true. He decided not to push the subject because if he pushed to hard things could blow up in his face. Knowing this was one thing, as long as Robert did not know it too.

Robert had finished counting the money. Seven hundred and fifty thousand dollars, this might actually turn into the final score he was hoping for. Calculating in his mind, he knew that Don stood to walk away from this with one hundred and seventy-five thousand for all his trouble. The seventy-five grand was his normal cut and the one hundred grand was for his assistance in all of this. It really did not matter; I stand to make five hundred and twenty-five thousand, not bad for ten days work. Granted, there had been a few new wrinkles added to his normal process but still to make over a half million dollars would be just fine. "Ok, stop playing with the money and let me see what you brought to this little party."

THE FINAL SCORE

Robert set the briefcase on the table and opened it up. Billy took a step back as he saw what was inside. He found himself looking at what he thought was at least ten kilos of coke. He had been told that a kilo was worth somewhere between one hundred and two hundred and fifty thousand dollars, street value. Take that times ten and he almost lost his balance as he came to the understanding that he stood to make in the neighborhood of two plus million dollars. Out of that profit, he could pay off the IRS and JD and not miss a lick. Damn his problems were truly over. He could not stop himself from laughing aloud.

Watching Billy, acting so smug, really pissed Robert off and he found himself wishing the end had already occurred. At that moment, Robert saw something out of the corner of his eye. Turning, he saw Bobby standing in the hall. Billy was so busy counting the money in his head he was going to make; he never saw what happened next. Just as Bobby stepped out of the hall, Robert heard the front door close. Looking past Billy, he saw Wayne and Henry step into the room behind Billy. The black man that had been holding Tina had seen Bobby and turning he pulled his gun. Bobby did not hesitate, with one loud bang the black man fell. As his body rolled onto his back, Robert saw a bullet hole in his forehead.

The look on Billy's face was pure horror. A friend of his had just had his head blown off and there was nothing he could do about it. He had told his friend that he did not need nor did he want a gun. It was just a drug deal, nothing more. Besides the dealer had befriended him, he had nothing to worry about. What with him and his brother there to make a show of force, why would he need a gun? With those thoughts going through his mind he suddenly realized that he had not seen the brother in some time. Where the hell is he and what is he doing? Did he not hear the shot that had just rang out in his living room? Billy was having trouble grasping what was happening.

About the time the shooting had sunk in, Billy sensed that someone was behind him. He turned just in time to see the fist that was going to hit the temple area of his head, but now it made flush contact with his jaw. Billy fell to one knee, obviously stunned by the hit. Spitting blood out of his mouth, he began to scream. Whatever he was trying to say made no sense. It was almost like he had lost the ability to speak the English language. This brought a smile to both Robert and Tina. Tina was in a mild case of shock, but she could understand that the people who had taken her hostage and had been holding her for the past few days were in dire trouble.

Trouble was an under statement. One was dead, she knew that for sure. One was on his knees spitting blood and the other was nowhere to be seen. I hope that he to was dead she thought. Suddenly another shot rang out. The man that had just hit Billy fell dead to floor. She would learn later that that was Wayne and the next to die was named Henry. Robert grabbed her around the shoulder and Tina screamed as if she had been shot. He pulled her close to his body and told her not to worry everything would be fine. Be fine she thought, people are being shot all around me, and you say things well be fine, what the hell had her boyfriend had been smoking she wondered.

Henry did not understand what was happening. Either Jorge or Don had just shot his best friend in the back. No this could not be true, someone must be behind them. But if there were someone behind them, what did he do, miss and hit Wayne. As he turned to try to figure out what the hell was going on he saw Jorge, gun in hand, and pointing it at Henry's chest. He tried to protest even though he knew it would do no good. Jorge seemed to pause and Henry had time to ask why. Jorge just looked at him, offering no explanation and pulled the trigger. As the blast was heard, Henry fell. He was not dead but he would be soon. Gasping for his last breath all Henry could do was look up at Jorge. Why had this happened? What had he done so wrong? Was this some kind of mistake? And with those thoughts, Henry breathed his last breath.

Now Tina was completely overwhelmed. Her knees were weak and if it were not for Robert holding her up she would also be on the floor. Robert, sensing this walked her to a chair. Sitting down Tina placed her head in her hands. She had no true idea as to what had just happened. Her head was spinning and she felt like she was going to throw up. Robert had moved away from her, where had he gone she wondered. Just then, someone was handing her a glass of water, taking the water she looked up and was glad to see it was Robert who was being so kind. There was some man standing next to him and they were talking but she could not hear a word that they were saying. The gunshots had been too close and her ears were not used to being subjected to anything that loud. Who ever this man is it was clear that Robert knew him and it appeared knew him well.

"So this is the young lady that you want to spend the rest of your life with," asked Don. Robert turned and smiling said, "Yes. What do you think?"

"Well, I must admit she is very good looking but I will hold back judgment until I can speak with her. But I must be honest, she appears to be more than I expected." Robert looked at Tina, and then back to Don and smiled as big as he could. "Yes sir, she is that and then some." This brought a chuckle to Don as he said, "To be with you for any period of time she better be that and then some." Hearing this gave Robert cause to laugh but it was cut short as Billy began to try to get to his feet only to be kicked back to one knee and more bleeding.

Bobby had walked over to where Don and Robert were standing and looking at Don he said, "Nice to see you boss." Don turned and asked if there had been any trouble. Bobby shook his head no and said, "I got here about ten. Made my way around back and found an unlocked door. Once I was inside there were no problems finding a place to hide. Honestly, it got rather boring waiting on you guys to show up. Did not know for sure why you had wanted me to wait but after seeing what happened to the two from Miami I guess it all makes sense. By the way, the other black man is dead in the back bathroom. I was taking a piss when the son-of-a-bitch walked in on me. Had to break his neck."

"Well at least you had something to entertain yourself with." Don said with a smile.

Now Billy had regained his composure and was again attempting to stand up. As he rose, he would flinch every time he thought he saw anyone near him move. Finally, he was fully erect but was still wobbly at best. Looking around at the carnage surrounding him, the expression on his face was blank. He turned to Robert and asked, "What the hell is going on?" Before Robert could say a word Don answered, "This is nothing more than the hell you brought on yourself." Billy turned to where the voice had come from and looking at Don, he inquired as to who he was. Now it was Robert's turn to say something. "Allow me to introduce the two of you. Billy, I am very pleased to introduce you to one of my closest friends, Mr. Don Volodchi from New York, New York." The look on Billy's face said it all. He knew the name, he had heard the reputation, and now here he was standing in Billy's living room, but why, he wondered.

The thoughts that were running through Billy's mind were doing so at such a speed he could not grasp even one. Looking at Don he said, "Mr. Volodchi it is so nice to finally meet you. I have heard so much about you and I must admit, you are one of the people that I have truly wanted to either meet or have you dine at my restaurant." Don looked at Robert with a look that said let us have some fun. "So Billy, why have you always wanted to meet me? I am truly curious." Billy appeared to be giving this some thought or he was simply trying to buy a few minutes. Finally he spoke, "I have followed your career through the papers and have always said that you are truly a self made man. I too started with nothing and have built a rather impressive business."

"So, am I correct in thinking that you seem to believe that we are two men of similar makeup?"

"Similar, I would have to say yes, in a way" responded Billy. This brought a strange grin to Don's face. "Billy, I trust I can call you Billy, please explain what you mean by that." Again, Billy needed to give this some thought. Before he spoke Don continued, "Should I assume that before you established yourself in your current profession you worked for men that you trusted and believed in. The type of men that you found yourself willing to put your life in their hands and theirs in yours. You found yourself doing things that you really did not understand but do them you did, without question." To this, Billy replied, "Yes exactly. I can easily say that the man I am is because of the men I have associated my self with in the past." Don turned and looked at Jorge as if to say he was impressed.

Continuing the dialogue with Billy Don now asked, "So Billy, if one of these men asked you to cause harm to one of their competitors you would do?"

"Well, yes I guess you could say that Mr. Volodchi."

"Please explain to me just exactly what you would do to bring this about," said Don. "Well sometimes I would just cut our prices and sometimes I would go as far to steal their employees away."

"Steal their employees that must have really caused some pain" Don said with a chuckle. In the background both Robert and Jorge got a laugh from Don's sarcasm. "If you have never been in the food service business you would have no idea just how painful something like that is. You see, when you lose a valued employee, one that has been with you for some time, it is not easy to go out just pluck someone off of the street to replace them." To this, Don continued his fun, "Oh I guess I could only imagine just how difficult that would be."

"Yes sir, if you have never been in that type of situation I am afraid to say, you really have no idea," responded Billy.

"I must say that the restaurant business must really be cut throat," Don continued. "You really have no idea" Billy replied. "You must be right, I have no idea. But listen Billy, if you have a few minutes, maybe I can pick your brain and learn a few things" Don inquired. Billy looked around, seeing three dead bodies he figured he would do just about anything to try to get in the good graces of Don Volodchi. "No sir, I really do not have anything pressing my time, so please ask whatever you would like" Billy stated in what for the first time was a clear and strong voice. It was clear to Don that Billy was beginning to relax and feel a bit of confidence about the situation he found himself in. "Well Billy, as I am sure you are aware, I do enjoy dinning out and have been thinking that since I spend so much money eating out, and maybe I should just buy my own place. What advice would you give someone like me who is thinking about this?" Billy gave this some thought before he responded with, "The first thing you must be aware of is the amount of time something like this requires. I mean owning your own place is similar to having a child. You see, it requires most of your time and all of your efforts. To stay with the child analogy, the child must learn to crawl before it walks and walk before it can run. Are you following what I am trying to say Mr. Volodchi?"

"Oh I think so. Correct me if I am mistaken, owning my own place would easily require me to put in what, something like nine to ten hours a day." This brought a slight smiled to Billy who replied, "I am sorry to tell you this Mr. Volodchi, but it would be more like twelve to fourteen hours each day and no less than six days a week. Assuming you would be open seven days a week."

"Oh my goodness, I had no idea it would take that much of my time. Please tell me more."

Billy was really beginning to think that he was doing more than simply buying time. He was beginning to think that if he played his cards correctly he might be asked to possibly be Mr. Volodchi's partner in such an enterprise. The more he thought about this he felt he could swing it. Sure, it would be difficult to be involved in two restaurants especially with one on each coast, but he could pull it off. Of course Mr. Volodchi would have to provide a place to call home while in New York, but hell he had millions and besides with the money he was going to make from selling the drugs if pushed he could afford to be involved in a venture like this. Even with the dead bodies, lying around him Billy was beginning to once again feel in control. After all, he was involved in a business conversation with the largest crime boss the country had known since Al Capone. Things were really starting to look up.

Allowing Billy to relax and gain some confidence was Don's plan. How he enjoyed fucking with people, especially self-centered assholes. He had done this so many times in his past. He, and only he, knew the outcome of this and oh, how he did enjoy it. As this was playing out in front of him, he began to remember a similar conversation with Robert. This conversation was the first the two had ever had. Robert was cocky and full of himself. The idea he had made some sense, but why would I be interested, Don remembered. He had sat and listened to this man talk about stealing money from drug dealers. It had reminded Don of his youth when he would hijack eighteen-wheelers that were full of cigarettes and be able to sell them on the street for pure profit. He knew it would only take one driver to be carrying a gun that could ruin everything for him. This was much like Robert's concern in dealing with the class of people he was dealing with. The more he listened the more he realized that this young man might be full of bullshit but then again he just might have hit on that one idea that could make him a fortune. Besides, he was offering me ten percent of whatever he got, Don remembered. And what is it I have to do, Don had asked. He was told really nothing at all. Just be around for a possible phone call and to allow this gutsy person to use my name if he ever found himself in a bad situation. Hell, this could be the easiest money I ever make, Don had thought that night. It was clear that he had been doing this for a while, so why not give this kid my blessings. Go ahead kid, use my name and give me a call if you need me to scare the hell out some fool. And thanks for the early payoff; I'll make sure it goes to a good cause, like me. And with that, the relationship between the crime boss and the kid from the Midwest was born. And like the child that Billy had spoke of, this relationship had truly matured. Don would never hesitate to tell others of this venture. He was proud of his decision and was proud of Robert. He had done everything he had said he would do that first night. Moreover and most importantly, he never delayed in bringing Don his ten percent. Damn it don't get no better than that, he thought.

Don brought himself back to the situation at hand, it was nice to remember things like this, but he had work to do, and he was never one who shrunk in front of work. Quickly he brought his mind back to Billy and said, "Other than the long hours, what else do I need to be aware of?" Billy looked directly at Don and said, "The next two areas of concern are those of labor and inventory."

"Labor and inventory?"

"Yes sir, labor and inventory. What I am talking about here is you need to make sure you control both of these areas and if you don't either one can bite you in the butt and both can drive you out of business faster than you may think."

"I think I understand the inventory part, meaning I don't want to be carrying, too much, but what are you talking about by labor."

"Well first off on inventory, you're half right. You do not want to be carrying too much, but the real problem lies in theft. You would be surprised to learn just how many steaks walk out the back door."

"Yeah, like someone is going to steal from me, of all people." This statement got a nice laugh from all listening. Billy smiled and said, "I see your point, Mr. Volodchi, but it does happen and I feel you just might be surprised to know just how ballsy some people can be. Now when it comes to labor, here you have to really watch what's going on. I mean you have to make sure that your sales are enough to support your entire labor cost. By entire cost, I talking about your kitchen staff, wait staff, bar staff, and of course your mangers. If this gets too out of whack you will be burning money just as if you where lighting a campfire with hundred dollar bills."

"Well I guess I see what your saying, there is a lot I need to look into before I make a decision like this" Don replied.

While this conversation was unfolding, Tina and Robert looked on in stunned amazement. Tina still had not recovered from the shootings that had taken place earlier, but finally she could hear, and Robert was surprised by Don's lackluster approach to Billy. He was really beginning to wonder just what Don was up to. Out of all the people involved in this, Billy was the one that Robert really wanted to be killed. He had no thoughts about the two black me killed by Bobby, he understood what Jorge had explained about Wayne and Henry but they were of no concern to him. Billy on the other hand was paramount in Robert's mind.

Tina just stood beside Robert attempting to recover from the earlier events. She had to be honest, she did not understand. But who were these other men. She had recognized Don Volodchi from the many pictures she had seen of him, in newspapers and television reports but who were the other two. She looked at Bobby and saw nothing she recognized. The same was with Jorge. It was easy to see that both men were associated with Mr. Volodchi, but how, she could not imagine. All she knew for sure was that the men who had been holding her for the past few days were all dead. Except for Billy, and he was talking shop with Mr. Volodchi, what the hell was going on she wondered.

Robert pulled her closer to his side and when she looked up at him, he bent down and gave her a kiss. Tina smiled and realized that this was the first kiss since she had been freed. At first, she wondered what had taken him so long, but after thinking about everything that had happened she understood. Robert leaned down and began to whisper in Tina's ear. "I am so glad you're alright. I have been so worried about what you were going through."

"I appreciate hearing that but listen to me mister, you have a hell of a lot to explain." Robert gave her a brief smile and then whispered, "I am sure we have a lot to talk about and we will certainly have plenty of time to do."

"Well, can you explain to me what the hell is going on right now?" she whispered. Robert gave this some thought and looked at Don as he continued to talk with Billy and had to say, "Honestly, I really don't know. Maybe Don is just trying to fuck with him."

"Don, you speak his name like he is some long lost friend" Tina said. "Well actually he is. We have known each other for about ten years now and trust me; he is a good friend to have. Just to let you know how good a friend he is, this whole day is thanks to him," Robert explained. To this, Tina looked at Robert in disbelief. "One day you will need to make sure I fully understand all of this" she exclaimed. Robert smiled and nodded his head. He fully understood the confusion that Tina must be experiencing at the moment, and he looked forward to spending time with her and making sure, she understood everything.

While Robert and Tina discussed things softly, Don and Billy continued their conversation about owning a restaurant. As the two continued to talk, it was easy for all to see Billy growing in confidence.

Now it was time for Don to move in for the kill. "So Billy, with everything you have explained to me, and I am grateful for you sharing your knowledge, I have one last question. Would you recommend that if I were to either buy a place or start out from scratch, in your opinion should I try to find a partner?" Hearing this question brought a smile to Billy's face. He thought he had just won the lottery. Maybe, just maybe, Don Volodchi was opening the door for him to walk through. How sweet it would be, to form a partnership with this man. Just how many doors would open for him, he wondered. Billy finally spoke, "Well Mr. Volodchi, taking a partner depends on several things. First, if you were unwilling to risk the amount of money it would take to either buy or open a place; a partner is warranted, to at least share the cost. Secondly, if that is the way you decided to go I must warn you that it is imperative to find someone you can truly trust. So, depending on your risk aversion and how much you wish to share with another my recommendation would be for you to most certainly take a partner." Don gave the appearance that he was giving these words considerable thought. Finally, looking directly at Billy, he asked "And what type of partner should I look for?" Billy not wanting to sound too interested said, "Mr. Volodchi, you must know tens if not hundreds of people involved in the restaurant business. Who am I do advise you on such an important decision?"

"Billy, don't sell yourself so short. Correct me if I am mistaken, you have been in the business for many years and have operated The Eatery for some time now and have been quite successful. Is this not true or have I been misinformed?" Billy, smiling said, "No Mr. Volodchi, you are correct. I have been in the business since my teens and yes The Eatery has been open for several years now and has been very successful."

"Well then, please answer my question." Giving this some thought Billy decided now was his chance and he did not want this chance to get away. He doubted he would ever be able to forgive himself if he blew this. "Don, may I call you Don?" Don simply nodded his head so Billy continued, "Thank you, Don, I would recommend that you find someone like me. Someone who has been in the business for a while, who truly understands what it takes to be successful, and of course someone you feel comfortable with and trust." Don smiled and said, "Billy are you saying that I should find someone like you or maybe I am hearing I should simply find you." Billy looked down trying his best not to appear too interested and looking back up at Don he said, "Far be it for me to ever assume that a man of your skills of reading people would ever think of turning to a west coast boy like myself to become a partner with you." This again brought a smile to Don and he said, "So, if I'm hearing you right you're telling me that it would be a mistake to try to talk you into becoming my partner."

"Oh no Don, if you are truly interested in forming a partnership with me, I am more than confident we can work everything out. As a matter of fact I would be honored to have the opportunity to be your partner in such of an operation." This caused Don to roar with laughter. The others joined Don in enjoying the moment.

Finally Don looked directly at Billy and began to speak, "Billy it appears to me that, and for reasons I can not begin to understand, you seem to think that you and I should form a partnership together. Why would you think that, I must ask myself? You have failed to understand the gravity of the situation. You have forgotten that the reason the two of us have even met is that you are in debt up to your eyeballs. You are so desperate that you have turned to a friend of mine in hopes of doing something, illegal I might add, to get your ass out of debt. And even though this was clearly explained to you, you could not be patient and let Robert do what he does best. And by that, I mean solve other people's problems. No you could not wait, so what did you do? You went out and kidnapped his fiancée. You have kept her here, and became emboldened to the point that you lectured Robert about who was in control. Does this sound as if a lot of trust is in play? I say no. Please explain to me how I should look at your actions over the past few days as someone that I would want to be in business with." Billy found himself becoming nervous again. He took a deep breath and said, "Well, I would hope that you would look upon me as a man that is willing to take risk and will do whatever it takes to get the job done." Again, Don laughed and said, "Take a chance and get the job done, is that what I am supposed to believe? What I see is someone who had no understanding of the situation he was involved in, and therefore had no idea as to how to get the job done. No I would have to say you would be the last person I would look at if I were looking for a partner."

"I understand why you would feel that way Mr. Volodchi but please allow me to explain myself in hopes that you will understand what I was thanking."

"Oh I think I understand everything very clearly. As your associate Pat explained things, you were intent to allow Robert to come here with the drugs you were trying to buy. Upon accomplishing that, you then intended to kill both him and his fiancée, take the drugs and get the cash that you needed to get out of debt. How am I doing so far?"

"Mr. Volodchi you can't believe what Pat said. He is always running his mouth about things he has no knowledge about."

"I can tell you one thing for sure, that is Pat will not suffer from that problem any more" Don said with a slight grin. "I had no intention of killing Robert or Tina. All I wanted to do was insure that he showed up with the drugs." Don shook his head and nodded to Bobby. Seeing this Billy turned towards him and saw that he had raised his gun. That was the last thing Billy would ever see.

Tina buried her head in Robert's chest and began to cry. Robert patted her head and tried to comfort her, the best he could. He did understand her reaction, but figured the best he could do was what he was doing. Don walked over and placing one hand on her back and told Robert, it was time to get her out of here. As the three began to walk out of the house, Don reminded Robert not to forget the money. Hearing this Robert returned to the table, picked the red duffle bag up, and then joined Tina and Don at the front door. It was the first time that he had noticed that the door had been closed the entire time. In seeing this, he quickly understood that due to the fact that no other house was within a quarter of a mile that it was unlikely for anyone to have heard the shots. Stepping outside he was surprised to see Jose standing by the Mercedes Benz, which was parked behind the stretch. As the three walked to the car, Don reached inside his suit and removed an envelope stuffed with cash. Handing it to Jose he said, "Thank you for picking these two up here at the La Brea Tar Pits." Jose smiled and nodded his head. He fully understood what this statement and the cash meant. He took the envelope and stuffing it in his pants pocket; he opened the passenger door for Robert and Tina. Don grabbed Robert by the arm and said, "I'll see you back in your suite. We have a few things left to do here." Robert nodded his head, he fully understood.

Watching the car pull away and head back towards the city Don smiled. He was happy that the two of them were back together and he had no doubt that Robert would be able to explain it all to her in a way that she would understand. Turning, he headed back inside the house, they had a few things left to do. Looking at Bobby he said, "Ok Bobby, make sure the only guns that are left have the fingerprints of the dead. We want to make sure that this looks just like a drug deal gone bad. We certainly don't want to give the cops any reason to look at this in other way. Any questions?" Bobby looked around and after surveying the situation said, he could make it happen. He took his time to make sure that each body had a gun that had been fired. He took careful time to assure that each gun only would show the dead mans fingerprints. Don watched his friend work. He had to admit that he did enjoy watching a master paint a perfect picture. Turning to Jorge he asked, "How do you think the one kilo we leave behind should look?" Jorge gave this some thought and replied, "With the way the bodies are laid out I think we can just leave one on the table. The only thing I question is there is no cash to be found, do you think that is wise?" Don smiled and said, "Why not. Would that not be a good reason for this whole thing to go so bad? One of these Miami boys showed up with the intention of unloading a kilo of coke and the buyer failed to have the money. And what with the two black guys coming from nowhere, all shit broke out." He patted him on the back saying, "Well it appears to be taken care of." With that, the three men walked out of the house and to their limo.

Inside Don asked Bobby if he had covered all his tracks getting to the house. Bobby smiled and said, "I took a cab to about five miles from here. Got out and walked the rest of the way. Got lucky, only saw one car and that was being driven by a little old lady with coke bottle glasses." Both Don and Jorge laughed when hearing this. As the car made its way to the Hilton, all three men sat back and relaxed. It had been a good day.

The ride back for Robert was anything but relaxing. He tried his best to engage Tina in small talk but she would have nothing of it. Instead, she just sat and stared out the window. At least she is holding my hand, Robert thought. At this point, anything that could be viewed as good was enough for him. At the hotel Jose opened the door to allow them to exit the car. He looked at Robert and said, "I hope the both of you enjoyed your visit to the Tar Pits" Robert smiled and shook his hand saying, "I'm sure we will see one another again, soon." Jose smiled and watched the two walk in the revolving doors. All he could do was wonder what they had been through, but being honest with himself he thought it probably was best he did not know.

As the two made their way through the lobby, Robert hoped that they did not appear to be too shook up. When they finally reached the suite, Robert went straight to the bar and fixed them each a drink. Handing one to Tina, who had already sat on the couch, he sat down in a chair across form her. Waiting for her to say something he sat and sipped his drink. Finally, Tina looked at him and began, "Why did all of this happen?" Robert took a deep breath and began explaining what Pat had done. He then went into how he called Don to request his help. He went into great detail about the conversation with Don, and how Bobby appeared the next day. When it came to the people from Miami, he could tell that Tina was not able to follow what he was saying. Recognizing this, he slowed down and repeated as much as he could remember. Tina seemed to understand; at least that was what he was wishing for. Looking at her glass, he realized that she had finished her drink.

Getting up and taking her glass, he returned to the bar and made her another. Returning to her, he handed her the glass but she grabbed his hand instead. Looking at him she said, "I think I understand what you have said. I have so many questions to ask but not now, please. I just want to sit here with you, happy to be here." Robert smiled as he sat down next to her. Looking into her eyes, he said there was one question he had to ask. Waiting for her response seemed like hours, but finally Tina took a sip of her drink and she told him to go ahead. Robert again took a deep breath and getting down on one knee he looked up at her and smiling he asked, "Tina, will you do me the honor of agreeing to marry to me?" Tina's eyes had already begun to fill with tears, she whipped them away and smiling said, "You bet your ass I will marry you!" The relief that Robert felt was so overwhelming he too began to cry. With tears running down his face he said, "Thank god, I so feared that I had lost you." Smiling, Tina brushed the tears away from his face and said, "It will take a lot more than being kidnapped, held hostage, and then seeing three men shot right in front of me to cause me to tuck my tail between my legs and run." Robert laughed and gave her one of the biggest hugs he had ever given anyone.

The two sat on the couch, enjoying each other's company and the drinks. After what had seemed like hours, there was a knock on the door. Robert went to open the door and as he did, Don walked inside. Walking over to Tina, he asked how she was and upon hearing that she was fine, he introduced himself to her. Tina graciously shook the mans' hand and said she was pleased to meet him. Don smiled and said, "I do wish we would have met under better circumstances. And I am sure you agree with that statement." Tina smiled and nodded her head. She really did, the circumstances that they had met were bad, and that was the understatement of all times, she thought.

Robert joined his best friends and in doing so, he handed Don a scotch. Don thanked him and sat down in one of the chairs across from the two of them. Finally he spoke, "The first thing I wish to do is raise my glass in congratulations on your engagement." Both Robert and Tina raised their glasses and Don was pleased to see the two of them smiling. After the toast Don continued, "I have to ask, have you guys set a date and determined a place for the big event?" Tina was quick with her reply, "Come on now, we have only been engaged for less than a week and unfortunately I have been away for a few days. So I am sure you will understand that we have not had the time to discuss a date, let alone a place." This brought a large laugh from Don. He smiled as he began to see that this young lady was very composed. He also thought that he would have to compliment Robert, as he described this girl perfectly. Glancing at his watch, Don excused himself to the bedroom saying he needed to make a call. Tina looked at Robert and just shook her head. She found it hard to believe that she was in the same suite with the largest crime boss known to the free world. Oh yes, Robert still had so much to explain.

After a few minutes Don came bounding out of the bedroom saying, "Our car will be downstairs within the next thirty minutes and we have dinner to enjoy. Robert leaned over and said, "Tina my love, I hope you enjoy Italian." Before she could say a word Don chimed in, "Of course she does, she is going to marry you is she not!" Both Tina and Robert laughed and hugged. Tina was surprised that this man, whom she only knew about through the news, was so down to earth. Sure, he wore only the best, but he had a nature about him that made it easy to feel comfortable and relaxed in his company. She had to remind herself who this man was, even with that thought; she had to say she liked him.

As the three made their way down to the lobby, Robert asked about Bobby. Don simply smiled and said that he was needed elsewhere and Robert knew not to ask any questions on the subject. Robert looked through the plate glass window and say Jose and the Benz. He smiled at seeing Jose; he was a good driver and one that understood his place. Getting in the car Don made sure Jose knew where they were headed. Jose smiled at Don and said, "Like there would be any other restaurant." Don smiled and patted his shoulder as he stepped in the car. Soon the car pulled up in front of Distefano's and the three were quick to get out.

Walking inside, Mr. Distefano was quick to greet them with the call of, "Welcome to my little place Mr. Volodchi and friends. We are so happy to see you and are blessed with your presences." This brought a smile to Don and all Tina could do was shake her head in disbelief. This man had been on the coast for only a couple of days and already had found a restaurant to call his own. She was not surprised to see all the tables were empty and knew that they would be seated in the middle of the dinning room. She glanced around the room and saw only two waiters, the others must have gotten an early night off she thought. No sooner than they had taken a seat when drinks appeared, almost magically Tina thought. Within a minute, the center of the table was cleared and a large platter of anti pasta was placed on the table along with several bottles of wine. Red of course, she thought. The wine was poured as the three began to select what they wanted off the platter and Mr. Distefano came by to make sure all were happy. He told them to relax and to enjoy the appetizer, as dinner was not quite ready. Don smiled as he poured each a glass of wine. Again, he raised his glass and offered a toast to their happiness and health. Robert and Tina raised their glasses and thanked Don for his thoughtfulness.

The food was excellent but Tina had to admit that she could eat no longer. Sitting back in her chair, she was amazed at the amount of food that these two men could put away. She had to wonder if this was what the rest of her life would be like. Robert had told her that he wanted to travel but he did mention how much he liked New York. How many of these dinners would they have in their future? As she had these thoughts, she soon realized that she really did not care, just as long as they included Robert. Watching them eat she started to think back over the past few days. She had dreamed that Robert would find someway to get her out of that house but she never would have imagined that in doing so he would have enlisted the help of Don Volodchi. No, there was no way she could have seen that one coming.

Dinner was over and they made their way to the car. Being settled inside Don turned to Tina and asked, "Did you enjoy Distefanos?" Tina smiled and said she had and thanked for asking and for dinner. Don waved this off as if it were his right to take them to dinner. Tina sat and watched the buildings go by as they made their way back to the Hilton. Upon arriving back, Don told Robert that he was going straight up to his suite as he had something's to take care of. He then told him that he would be by around ten in the morning so that they could wrap up their business. Robert smiled and thanked Don for all he had done and told him he would see him in the morning. As they got to the elevator, Tina grabbed Roberts hand to hold him back. Don gave the two a smile, said, "Behave yourself!", and with that disappeared in the elevator. Tina pushed the up button and told Robert, "I just wanted to be alone with you." Robert smiled as the doors opened.

Tina could not keep her hands off Robert. The two hugged and kissed all the way to their floor. As they entered the suite, Robert offered to make them each a nightcap and Tina just shook her head no. She told him to sit down and she would be right back. With that, she headed towards the bedroom and closed the door behind her. Robert sat down and began to replay the events of the day in his head. In doing so, he turned the television set on in an attempt to discover if the scene had yet been discovered. Much to his disappointment there was nothing about it on the news. Just as he turned the set off the bedroom door opened. Tina came out wearing the most beautiful and sexy negligee he had ever seen. All he could do was smile. This was exactly what Tina had been hoping for and she grabbed his hand and led the way back into the bedroom. With the lights out, it was still easy for the two of them to find the bed.

Robert got out of bed and looked at the clock; it showed it was eight thirty in the morning. He stepped out into the living area and called room service. He ordered coffee and the fruit bowl that Tina so enjoyed. Hanging up the phone, he smiled as he did enjoy doing the little things that made her happy. With that taken care of, he headed to the shower. After he had gotten dressed, he stepped back into the bedroom to discover that she was gone. He was quick to make his way to the living room as he was not yet comfortable not having her close by. He smiled when he saw her lying on the couch still wearing her negligee. As he approached, he tossed a cover on her, which caused her to laugh. "What, I can only wear this at night?" she playfully asked. Robert smiled, "That it was fine but room service was on its way and he would prefer not give the guy that kind of a tip." Tina laughed but she had to admit to herself, this just made her love him that much more.

They were soon enjoying the coffee and fruit when a knock sounded on the door. Robert looked at his watch and said, "Just like Don, right on time." Opening the door, he allowed Don to step in and offered him a cup of coffee. Just as he said yes, Tina made a fast exit to the bedroom. Most of the men Robert knew would have had something to say but not Don. No, he had too much class for that, Robert thought. The two men sat down with their coffee and turned the television set on. Checking the on screen guide, they found an all news channel that only reported on events in L.A. After a few minutes, they heard the reporter begin to talk about something horrible that had been discovered in the hills overlooking the city. He went on to describe the scene the police had found after someone had reported the owner of an upscale restaurant had not shown up as he normally did for the evening business. The reporter continued to talk about how the police had found five men dead in the restaurant owners' house. It seemed that three of the men were from L.A. and the other two appeared to be form the Miami area. The police reported that it appeared to be a drug deal gone badly as they found an unopened kilo of cocaine on a table and that the bodies were distributed around the living area. When asked, the police spokesperson said that the department felt that there was no need to look much further than the scene already mentioned, as it all looked very plain and easy to understand. Don turned to Robert and said, "Damn, that Bobby sure knows what he is doing." Robert smiled and said, "Have to agree with that, must have had a good teacher." With that, both of the men enjoyed a good laugh. As Tina came back into the living room, she asked if anything had been on the news. Robert gave a brief account of what they had heard and Tina offered a sigh of relief.

THE FINAL SCORE

After turning the set off Robert got up and went to the bedroom. When he came out, he was holding the money that he owed Don. Don took the money, gave it a quick look over, and agreed that it was the correct amount. Then he pulled what appeared to be a silk purse out of this pocket and put the money inside of it. Putting the purse next to him in the chair, he turned and asked Tina if there was any coffee left. Tina smiled and said she would check and if not she would order some more. She was soon reaching for the phone, as the carafe was empty. Sitting down next to Robert, she looked at Don and asked, "What do you have planned for today?" Don smiled and replied, "I have a flight back to New York this afternoon so as soon as we finish everything up here I am headed to LAX." The three of them made small talk, mostly about what Tina had endured over the past few days. No one was happier than Tina was when the knock came on the door.

After pouring each a cup, she returned to her seat next to Robert and Don began to speak. "Listen you two, you have to promise that you will not go and get married without me being there. I expect to be right there to observe the official beginning of your lives together. Now you must understand that if I am not there I will be extremely upset. And Tina, Robert can attest to the fact that I am probably the last person on earth you want to cause to be extremely upset." Both Robert and Tina laughed at Don's faked frankness and it took all he had not to join them in their laughter. After they had regained their composure he continued, "Robert I know you have already told me that this was going to be your final score. I understand what it means to have gotten to a point where retirement can be realized, and no longer dreamed about. However, I must ask you this one thing. I must know that if I ever need you that all I will have to do is call." Upon hearing this, a small lump grew in Roberts's throat. It was the first time in ten years that Don Volodchi had ever made such a request. Before he spoke, he stood up, an attempt to show the respect he felt for this man, and said, "Mr. Volodchi I would hope that you would know all you would ever have to do, in the event you needed me, would be to call. Sir, the only thing you would ever need to do is make sure I know." This brought a rather large smile to the face of Don Volodchi. He would never be able to express how these words made him feel. It was true, just as Jorge had assumed, he loved this man like no other. He felt that they were two in the same. Self made, valued friendship, and took whatever they saw that they wanted. It was truly a shame that his friend was Irish. God how he wished this were not true, but it was and it just had to be accepted. He was a strong man, the leader of his family, but this was something that not even he could pull off. No, there was no way that this Irish pug could be made. Nevertheless, one thing was for sure, all of his people knew the love that he felt for him and they knew that he was welcomed just like he was family.

After clearing these thoughts from his mind, he stood and smiled at Robert. Turning he asked Tina to stand next to Robert. As she did, Don placed his cup on the table and picked up the silk purse. Looking straight into Tina's eyes he smiled and said, "Tina I have a gift for you. I want you to understand that this is for you, as I don't ever want to hear that you have ever wanted for anything." With that being said, he placed the purse in her hands. He then turned to Robert and said, "Take care of this woman my friend, she is a real one!" He then grabbed Robert by the shoulders and kissed him on each cheek. And with that, he made his way to and out of the door.

Robert and Tina stood in the room absolutely speechless. The generosity of Don Volodchi had taken them both by complete surprise. All Tina could do was look at the money in the purse. Finally, she began to laugh and it soon became apparent that she was not going to be able to stop. All Robert could do was hold her tightly against his body and whisper in her ear how much he loved her. Soon they made their way back to the bedroom.

Tina awoke to discover that Robert was no longer in bed. Stepping into the living room, she saw him on the couch and asked, "Who gave you permission to get out of bed?" Robert laughed and said, "I did not know I had to ask permission!" Tina gave him a little laugh as she kissed him and sat on his lap. "And what have you been up to my dear?" she asked. Robert smiled and said, "Nothing much, but you have one hour to shower, pack, and be ready to leave."

"And where are we going?"

"Aruba" was the only word that Robert spoke. Tina felt the air escape from her lungs. As she regained her breath, she looked into his eyes and smiled and said, "I have no suitcase." All Robert did was point with his left hand and when she turned to look, she saw a whole set of luggage by the bar. Smiling she said, "Well someone has had a busy afternoon." Robert nodded his head, asked if she like the luggage, and was pleased to find out, she did.

Soon they were on the plane heading towards Aruba. Tina felt like the whole day had flown by in a millisecond. It seemed like they had just gotten up to coffee and fruit but so much had happened. They had learned the thoughts of the police in regards to what they had found at Billy's, they had received the blessing of Don Volodchi, had made love again, and now they were flying to a wonderful Caribbean island with plans to really jump start their lives together. As they sat in First Class sipping champagne Tina thought she could really get used to this.

Getting into a limo at the airport, Tina asked what hotel they would be staying. Robert just looked at her and smiled. As they made their way through the streets, Tina did her best to try to see what was outside. Finally, she gave it up it was just too dark. Sitting back in the seat, she closed her eyes and began to examine just how much her life has changed in such a short period of time. For the first time in her life, she was happy and did not feel like she had anything to worry. The man that was making her so happy seemed to be able to take care of anything. And if not, at least he had friends to call. Suddenly the car pulled onto what appeared to be a long driveway. As they made their way up a house came into view. There were lights on everywhere. The car came to a stop and her door was opened. Standing outside was an elderly man who offered her a hand. Stepping outside she tried to focus her eyes to see more than the lights from the house. This proved to be impossible. The man who had helped her from the car began to speak, "Good evening Mr. Robert, it is so good to have you home again. I will make sure all of your bags are in the master room and my wife has made drinks for the two of you." Robert said thank you and grabbed Tina by the hand.

Turning to look at him, she asked, "Home?" He laughed as he said it was just a little place and it was so much better than any hotel room. Tina laughing said, "A small place, with live in servants, damn I wish the sun was up so I could really take it all in."

"In due time my love, in due time." With that, they made their way inside. They were greeted with a warm hello from the woman who had been waiting for them. They later learned that the two caretakers had been waiting ever since they got the call from Robert. They both were so glad he was back and seemed to like the idea that he was no longer alone. After drinks, Robert led Tina to the master room and when the door was opened, Tina again felt her breath escape her body. It was by far the largest bedroom she had ever seen. Her first thought was to make sure Robert did not leave her as she could easy never find him in here. All Tina could do was smile and fight back the tears. Robert suggested they get some sleep as he planned for them to be swimming with the dolphins in the morning.

At breakfast, Tina was excited about what Robert had said last night. "Swimming with the dolphins, is this something you usually do with all the girls you bring down here?" Robert turned very slowly to her and said, "Yes my love swimming with the dolphins, and no Tina, you are the first person I have ever brought down here." Tina could not believe what she had just been told. Her smile said otherwise, but she had no reason to doubt what he had said. However, her mind kept working, this place is too nice, too special, to have never shared it before this. Robert could sense what she was thinking. He reached over, took her hand in his, and said, "You need to understand that this place has always been my escape. I have come here often to celebrate but because of what I used to do, I have been forced to celebrate my victories alone. I also ask that you understand or at least try to understand just how happy I am to have you with me." All Tina could do was smile.

Having finished breakfast and changing into swimwear, they made there way down to the water. Stretched out before them was the bluest water Tina had ever seen with her own eyes. They walked out on a wharf that seemed to extend at least one hundred yards. As they approached the end, Tina could see several dolphins that seemed to be waiting on them. She was as excited as a child would be on Christmas morning, she could no longer wait and she broke into a slight jog and quickly dove in. Robert laid their towels down as he watched her frolicking with the mammals that had indeed been waiting. The last thing he did was to make sure his phone was safe on the towels before he dove in to join Tina and the dolphins. As he swam with his love and played with the dolphins, he heard his phone ringing.